Aurora's Amulet

An Atlas Cliffs series prequel

Angela van Liempt

Dawn Publishing

First paperback edition May 2025

Cover design and Aurora silhouette image by Gigi Creatives at https://www.instagram.com/heygigicreatives/

Maddie and Enid chapter header art by Whitney Law at https://www.instagram.com/newinkbookservices/

Editing by Kayla Ramoutar

Formatting by Angela van Liempt

ISBN 978-1-7782544-8-2 (Paperback)

ISBN 978-1-7782544-9-9 (E-book)

Published by Dawn Publishing

www.dawn-publishing.com

*Ro Jr., thanks for motivating me to "lock-in" and keep writing
when I needed a 'Joggins' pep-talk.
Now to find the perfect sign for my book wall with this phrase...*

"How brave the moon shines in her skin; outnumbered by the stars."

Angie Weiland-Crosby

PROLOGUE

AURORA - 1887

The sea crashed against the rocks of Neptune Point with a thunderous roar, its spray colliding with the air. A chilling premonition settled into her bones as Aurora made her home in Atlas Cliffs. Dreams haunting her nights revealed a fate that would alter the course of magic. Would she be the one chosen to forge a new path brimming with untold power for those to follow?

Confronting a tumultuous past where magic and healing powers were deemed witchcraft, she had concealed her mystic abilities from the dark wrath lurking from beyond the grave. The spirit haunted this place as though he'd been waiting for her.

Hunting her.

Yet, love had found her, and her legacy would carry on in her children. She would not rest until she secured the future of her own daughter, safeguarding the mystics who would inevitably call this town home.

A narrow pathway of water slowed into a wide ripple as it flowed from the forest where the Coda River met the ocean in perfect harmony. Its current carved channels into the soil deep within the ground, where all things begin and end. This was where the full moon's silver light aligned with a hidden pathway to a concealed entrance, promising passage for the soulless to another realm, its door sealed with an impenetrable lock.

Indeed, magic *breathed* here. The place where darkness meets the light and light shall always prevail.

Aurora shielded her eyes with a gloved hand as the sun reflected off the ocean, and beams of light illuminated the iron railing encircling the lighthouse beacon. The work was complete, and the looming tower would one day carry her namesake. Her fingers instinctively grasped the black jewel dangling from a silver chain around her neck. Magic pulsed like a heartbeat beneath her skin, responding to her silent command as a spell of protection surrounded her. She had harnessed the Sisterhood. As promised in a vision, the talisman was returned to her, hidden in the attic of the Keeper's house the day she moved in with her family. Their magic contained inside the jewel would protect her home.

The white paint gleamed under the sunlight of the two-story Keeper's house, and an untouched heap of freshly cut wood had been piled in the backyard for the stove.

Home.

The cold air bit her face, and she released the onyx jewel, clutching her wool coat tighter. Her hand fell to rest over her growing bump, concealed by the layers of her dress and petticoat.

The amulet pulsed with warmth, sending a scorching sensation along her skin as magic burned within her, its power escalating. The breeze swirling from the sea carried whispers from beyond the veil to her ears.

Breathe life.

She inhaled the salty ocean air as love surrounded her. For the moment, time was in her hands, and she reveled in creating a life for her family. She thrived as a woman, a wife, a mother, and part of the Sisterhood, protecting those who could not save themselves. She was living her purpose, and a profound sense of peace filled her soul.

Gathering the skirts of her dress in her hands, she entered the lighthouse. Releasing the layers of fabric, she ran her fingers along the concrete walls as she climbed the winding staircase. Her refusal to wear a corset allowed her to move freely... and *breathe.*

As her hand closed around the cold, iron railing, a thread of purple light enveloped the amulet, and a metallic tang invaded her mouth, akin to the taste of blood. She tugged the silver chain, freeing the jewel over her coat, and a vision of the future unfolded in her mind. She drew shallow breaths as the image of a young woman with flaming red hair adorned in a dress the shade of the deepest azure flashed behind her eyes. A shadow loomed in front of the woman, engulfing her in a gray mist as it moved with a jerky, unsettling grace. Fear shrouded the woman's face, and she held her hands up in defense. Hands that burned with *light.* Aurora relinquished her grasp on the railing and covered her mouth to suppress a scream as the fleeting glimpse disappeared.

The vision was anchored in the future, but its precise time remained unclear. Time flowed with the speed of sand cascading through an hourglass. Whether ten years or one hundred years from this moment, time did not matter in the soul realm. But there would be others who walked the line between life and death, with the power to guide the souls of the departed to their place of belonging, and their lives would be woven within Atlas Cliffs like gold threads in a tapestry.

Clinging to thoughtful determination, she ascended the winding staircase. Excited discussions of wind directions and the use of kerosene to light the beacon, steering ships from harm's way, grew louder as Aurora rounded the top of the stairs. A sensation of tingling covered her skin as her husband's calm voice rose above the others gathered in the lantern room. He was a gentle soul who loved her with unconditional abandon.

Heat tickled Aurora's face and down her neck to her fingertips. Ribbons of light spun deep within the amulet, and she tucked it beneath her squared neckline, hiding it from view. Folding her arms across her chest, she watched the men, their chests puffed as they slapped each other on the back, boasting about their magnificent creation.

"Mama!" Breaking free from her father, their daughter ran into her mother's embrace, and Aurora kissed her head.

"Aurora." Her husband's dark eyes sparkled with pride, and she extended a gloved hand as one of the local news reporters angled a wooden box to photograph the moment. "This shall serve as our home by the sea." His smile broadened as he lifted her hand to his lips, leaving a trail of warmth on her skin underneath her knit gloves.

He released her hand, and her heeled boots echoed as she sauntered onto the landing, leaving their daughter in his care. Seagulls screeched overhead, their cries piercing above the surge of waves against the rocky shore. Icy air swirled up from below, encircling her in a frigid embrace, and her body stiffened. Her hand dropped to cradle her stomach as her other hand grasped the silver chain, freeing the amulet from beneath her collar. Golden threads emanated from the jewel's core and crept along the surface of the stone like the roots of a tree settling into the depths of the earth.

I am not alone.

A man's figure, shrouded in gray smoke, stood at the bottom of the lighthouse. His hood fell back as he extended a hand to point at her, his lips curling into a malevolent smirk. She tightened her woolen coat around herself and met his gaze, refusing to turn away despite the tension consuming her body. As the sea churned around him, the sand spun faster through the narrow passageway of time in the proverbial glass.

When I choose to leave this existence, it will be on my terms, and mine alone.

Emanating an aura of death, his hands were stained crimson with the blood of innocents. He pursued mystics, aware of their imminent magical presence. Aurora silently promised never to rest until the spirit who embodied darkness met a fate sealed with an eternal death.

Part One
1985

Maddie Harlow

ONE

MADDIE 1985

A mournful howl sliced through the forest and a gust of wind shook the tent, nestled underneath a thicket of trees.

Maddie hesitated, her lips lingering on Aiden's. "What was that?" She broke away from his embrace and sat up. The sleeping bag slid down, leaving her bare arms covered in goosebumps.

Aiden rolled onto his back, tucking his hands behind his head. "We're in the middle of the woods, Mads, could be anything." He rubbed her back, but his touch failed to ease the tension creeping into her shoulders. "How many times have we come here camping, and nothing bad has ever happened? Haven is safe, anything out there is more afraid of us than we are of it."

As Maddie unzipped the tent door, a rush of crisp air, carrying the pungent scent of pine and damp earth, swept through the mesh screen. The fire had long since burned down to embers, casting an orange glow as it succumbed to the chill of the fall night. Moonlight filtered through the trees, illuminating shadows that disappeared along the path leading away from Haven.

A sudden gust of wind tore through the trees, sending bare branches scraping each other. The sounds of the forest had never evoked fear before, but tonight, for the first time in Neptune Point, she couldn't shake a feeling of ominous dread.

People wouldn't understand if they knew who Maddie really was. If they ever discovered her strange ability for coaxing plants to bloom in impossible places at impossible times of the year, or found out she could miraculously breathe life into a dying butterfly with the touch of her fingers... if anyone knew she could predict when death was near, they would ostracize her and her family, and she'd rather die than allow that to happen to Aiden and Gabe.

But lately, there was something about this place that magnified her magic, plaguing her with premonitions of darkness beyond her control.

"I don't want to come here anymore," she whispered.

"I thought you loved it out here?" Aiden's hand dropped from her back to the sleeping bag. "We've waited ten years to have a night alone again, thanks to Nellie looking after Gabe." A laugh escaped him, and he caught himself when his gaze fell on Maddie's face.

A crawling sensation trailed down the back of her neck as the wind shook the towering pines along either side of the Coda River, and the churning rapids echoed louder. This place had always been the escape from town Maddie cherished, but nature's whispers turned to warnings, filling her with an unexplained fear she'd never experienced before.

"Something's different, Aiden. We made a mistake coming tonight."

Aiden sat upright and peered through the screen mesh. "I've made mistakes in my life, but going anyplace with you will never be one of them."

Another howl resounded in the distance, and barren tree branches creaked as a rush of air swept up fallen leaves. Maddie twisted her hair around her fingers until they became numb. "Someone's out there."

"Okay." Aiden tugged his boots on and grabbed a flashlight as he unzipped the screen door. He stepped outside and dead leaves crunched under his feet. "Pass me my jacket, love."

Yanking a thick knitted sweater over her head, Maddie grabbed his plaid work coat and crawled out of the tent to stand beside him.

"See?" He angled the light around the tree line, casting shadows as leaves rustled. "It's just us out here. Nothin' to be afraid of."

A shrill buzzing pierced her ears as a shadow darted through the trees. "Let me see that." With her eyes fixed on the trail up ahead, she took the flashlight from Aiden and crept forward.

Leaves scattered across the forest floor, landing on frost-covered moss with every step she took away from the tent. Shoving branches aside, she followed the shadow into the woods. The frigid breeze carried a hushed voice—a woman's voice. A sudden pungent aroma turned her stomach, smelling of burning flesh and hair.

"What are you doing?" Aiden called out from the trail.

She spun around and shone the light in his direction. "Can you smell that?"

He pushed his red hair out of his eyes. "Pine needles and rotting wood?"

"Something's burning." As she stepped over a fallen tree, she slipped, losing her grip on the flashlight, grasping a branch to keep from falling. The shadow darted past her and the sickening smell intensified. She released the branch and stumbled, crashing to the ground. Dampness seeped into her pants and the back of her sweater, chilling her skin.

"You okay?" Aiden trudged through the dense brush, leaning down to gather her in his arms as he lifted her off the ground. "There's nothing but animals out there, love." With an arm around her waist, he retrieved the flashlight, and its beam cut through the darkness, leading the way back to the uneven trail.

Her shallow breaths created plumes in the surrounding air, and she shivered as she brushed dirt off herself and picked leaves out of her tangled hair. The woman's voice fell silent, and the crisp fall air with a hint of chimney smoke replaced the nauseating smell, but something was very wrong.

"Take me home, I want to go home."

Aiden stood in front of her, the warmth of his hands radiating through the thick sweater as he rubbed her arms. His fingers gently brushed against her chin, tilting her face to meet his gaze. "Then we'll go home. Let's pack up."

Taking her hand, he led her back to the tent. Inside the nylon A-frame cocoon, she rolled up her sleeping bag and stuffed her things into the backpack they shared. Aiden packed the disassembled tent into a canvas bag and slung it over his shoulder. The glow from the flashlight perched on a nearby log cast just enough light that Aiden's green eyes sparkled as he looked at her.

"Whatever's got you spooked, it's gonna be okay. It's just a sign our camping days are over... for now, anyway." A mischievous smile crossed his face. "We'll just have our dates at home by the fire after Gabe's asleep like we always do."

Home.

Atlas Cliffs would always be their home. She cradled his face in her hands. "It's late. When we get home, I want you to hold me and never let go." She kissed him, lingering on his lips as he hugged her in a tight embrace.

Leaning back, he brushed strands of her wind-blown hair off her forehead, but his expression turned serious. The lines at the outer corners of his eyes deepened, etched with the laughter, tears, and every moment of life they'd shared, making him appear older than his thirty-five years.

"No regrets?" he asked.

"None."

"Let's go home, love."

Maddie adjusted her backpack and trudged along the narrow pathway toward the truck, with Aiden following close behind. She wanted no part of the warning creeping under her skin and didn't pause or strain to hear the whispers again.

She had always dismissed the local legend of Aurora's cursed lighthouse, but something in the woods tonight made her doubt everything she believed.

As she reached the top, emerging from the dense pine trees, the rhythmic sweep of the lighthouse beacon cast a glow over the rocky shore below, and curls of smoke spiraled from the Keeper's house at the bottom of the hill. A sweet hickory aroma filled the air, replacing the eerie burning odor that had turned her stomach moments earlier.

Aiden tossed the packed tent and sleeping bags into the truck bed before sliding the backpack from her shoulders. "Let me lighten your load." He smiled as he placed it in the truck.

"Ever the gentleman, aren't you?"

"Not near enough." Aiden climbed into the driver's seat. He muttered about picking up Gabe from Nellie's in the morning and taking him to the market for breakfast, but the crashing waves below drowned out his words.

Leaving the passenger side door open, Maddie ventured away from the truck and took a few steps down the sloped hill. Darkness filled the windows of the large, two-story Keeper's house, except for light flickering from a large picture window on the bottom level. White paint curled down the sides, revealing bare wood underneath, and one side of the porch sank to the ground. A powerful squall blew off the ocean, tossing her hair against her face. She wiped the strands from her lips, leaving a salty taste lingering. Rare glimpses of the man who maintained the lighthouse unnerved her. It wasn't his disheveled appearance that bothered her, but the way he scrutinized her, always with a solemn expression on his weathered face, and always wielding an axe with a pipe in his mouth.

"Maddie? Something's... wrong." Aiden called above the rumbling truck's engine, and she spun around as he stepped out of the truck and gripped the door frame.

"Aiden? Aiden!" She rushed to his side as he collapsed on the ground. Her pulse thumped in her ears as she dropped to her knees. Gripping his shoulders, she turned him over, letting his head fall into her lap.

"Where does it hurt? Can you breathe? Please look at me." She placed her fingers along his neck, but his pulse was erratic, and he gasped in shallow breaths. "Don't die, don't die, don't leave me." She couldn't hide her building panic as she positioned herself over him.

His hand rose to clutch his chest and sweat beaded along his pale face. He opened his eyes and looked at her. "It hurts like someone dropped a boulder on my chest, am I having a heart attack?" His body slumped, but his chest heaved with desperate, strangled breaths.

Her composure shattered, and her body trembled as she hovered over him. She took several deep breaths, but her heart still pounded in her chest like a drum. She'd learned CPR once in high school, but that was years ago. Placing her hands on his chest, she pressed down, counting with each burst of pressure. How many chest compressions? Breaths? The hospital was a half hour drive away—what if they didn't make it in time and he died on the ride there? No, she couldn't let herself spiral out of control. Aiden would not die. She could run down the hill to the Keeper's house and use his phone. Fear's grip tightened like a knot inside of her, but a sudden metallic taste of magic coated her tongue, reminding her of who she was.

Breathe life.

The spell she'd used many times, saving wounded birds who had slammed into the window, or a butterfly that had lost its ability to fly, calmed her mind.

"Mads..." Desperation laced Aiden's wavering voice, and he released a sharp cough as his body shook.

She knew what she had to do. The secret she'd kept buried for so long clawed its way to the surface, leaving her with no other option.

I will not let him die.

She exhaled and a burst of sparkling warmth rushed along her skin, settling into her hands like balls of fire. She brushed her fingertips along his graying cheeks, recoiling at the chill of his skin. As she placed her palms against his chest, the heat radiated around him in a bright purple glow she'd never seen before. His breaths came in frantic gasps as his heart raced beneath her touch, and his agony seeped into her hands like vines constricting around her fingers.

"Listen to me, my love, you will not die tonight," she said between choked sobs. "Fight your way back to me." She focused, summoning her magic to take over and save his life. "Call the quarters, seek shelter from the storm, seek bravery in the face of death," her voice wavered, but she continued reciting the spell. "Breathe life."

The earth underneath her thrummed with powerful energy, and the woman's voice returned, repeating the spell with Maddie's. Searing magic coursed through her like the current of the river flowing to the ocean, pressing against her skin like it would rip her apart, but she kept her hands pressed against him. The air shimmered as a flash of purple surrounded her, transforming into ribbons of light that wrapped around Aiden.

His body relaxed, and his breathing slowed to a gentle rhythm. The tightness gripping her fingers unraveled, and the magic wove its way through him, breathing life into his chest. The light vanished, leaving behind a steadying heartbeat as his deathly ashen face flushed and regained a healthy glow.

She flung herself on him, kissing his face and holding him as tears soaked the collar of his shirt. "I did it, you're back."

As the magic faded, the biting cold returned. Aiden sat up, wrapping his arms around her. "What happened? Did I pass out?" he rasped.

"Don't you remember? You called out to me, you were in pain, you were..."

Dying.

"I what? Did I faint?" He pulled his hands from around her back and rubbed his face. "I don't think I've ever passed out like that before, are you all right, love?"

He doesn't remember.

Standing, she extended her hand and helped him up, but he was steadier than she expected him to be as he leaned against the front of the truck. "How long has it been running?"

"Not long." She couldn't take her eyes off him. Her magic had worked on a person. What would that mean for her? For her family?

"We should get home." He ran his fingers through his red hair, brushing dirt and seagrass away.

"Aiden?"

He turned to face her as he approached the driver's side, and she ran into his waiting arms.

"Hey, it's okay, I'll be fine." He caressed her face and kissed her forehead. "Looks like we're not alone," he said.

Breaking away from him, she followed his gaze.

The front door of the Keeper's house swung open, and the man stepped onto the front porch. He surveyed each side of the house before lifting his head, locking eyes with her. As the untamed strands of his white hair blew around his chin, they caught the faintest glimmer of light, making him look almost otherworldly against the darkness. She could offer a friendly wave. After all, it was almost midnight, and they were on his property... or she could continue staring at him like a judgmental local, even though that was the last thing she'd want to be.

The man leaned against his house, slipping his hands into his pockets as he observed her, but she couldn't tear her eyes away from him. A barrage of whispers filled her ears, belonging to the woman who had just helped save her husband from sure death, but when Maddie searched for the source of the sound, no one else was around.

Leaving Aiden by the truck, she ventured closer to the house.

"What are you doing?"

"I just want a closer look," she said.

Did the man in that house know what had happened? What if he could hear the woman, too?

As the truck's headlights faded from view, she slowed her pace, hesitant to leave Aiden alone. With a quick nod, the man disappeared back inside his house, closing the door behind him, and the light behind the curtains flickered off.

Driven by a sense of urgency, she knew she needed to come back and meet the man in that house. She had to learn whatever he knew about the secrets of this place.

"Maddie?" Aiden called.

"I'm coming." As she headed back to the truck, a trail of white lilies bloomed at her feet, illuminating a path through the sea grass and sand. She halted, her head tilting upward as Aiden stood waiting for her.

With her breaths fogging around her in the cold air, she bent down to touch the delicate blossoms. The flowers defied the frosted ground, growing against the odds in a place where they shouldn't be thriving, and despite her magic, she had never witnessed such a thing in her life.

Did I make this happen?

A sudden burst of crimson, like blood splatter on silk, stained the petals of the largest flower near her foot. She lifted it from the sand, and a tingling sensation traveled from the flower to her fingers. The woman hummed a haunting lullaby in her ear, and a soft, purple light illuminated the flower before it crumbled into fine, powdery dust in her hand. The flowers around her feet surrendered, retreating into the earth as their radiance disappeared.

A brick of fear settled in her stomach. Could the curse of Aurora's lighthouse be real? The murmuring voices of Atlas Cliff's locals filled with legends of troubled souls wandering Neptune Point dating back centuries bombarded her mind.

Maddie wiped her hands on her coat and broke into a run, her heart racing and her lungs burning.

Aiden opened her door, but as she gripped the seat to climb inside the safety of the truck, the woman's voice intensified, obliterating every other sound, including Aiden's questions.

"Welcome to the Sisterhood, Madeline Harlow." The calm voice sent warmth cascading from Maddie's head to her toes inside her boots. The woman's ethereal voice continued, "A gift is waiting for you when you are ready to claim it."

A metallic taste lingered on Maddie's tongue again, and a burning sensation coursed through her palms as Aiden closed the door and strolled to the driver's side, leaving her alone in the cab of the truck.

She would have lost him tonight if it hadn't been a shift in her magic, somehow magnified by an unseen force living here, at Neptune Point. She shuddered and turned her head toward the window as tears pricked her eyes. Her family was everything and losing Aiden or Gabe... She didn't believe surviving a loss like that was possible.

Aiden steered the truck onto the road and glanced over at her as she clasped her hands together in her lap. "I think you're right," he said. "Something isn't right here tonight."

She reached her hand over the center console and laced her fingers with his. "I love you."

"Always, love." With his focus on the road, he raised her fingers to his lips and kissed them. "The man down there might be unusual, I'll give you that, but he's probably just lonely and harmless." He yawned as he drove over the bridge, away from Neptune Point.

Away from the lighthouse, its keeper, and the whispers from beyond the grave.

Two

MADDIE 1985

Late fall brought darkness early, and light from the full moon streamed through the kitchen window. The wind-up timer jangled, and Maddie turned off the oven, taking out a tray of pastries. Wiping her hands on her apron to rid them of flour, she sauntered closer to the back door and peered through the sheer curtains.

It had been a week since the night at Neptune Point, but even with November's brisk arrival and the summer long gone, the gardens surrounding her house defied logic and shifted from their deadened state into vibrant life. She'd covered them with burlap to hide the glowing blooms from prying eyes until she could get the new and unusual magic surging through her under control. Her hands weren't visibly red, but intense heat tingled over her skin like a sunburn, and no amount of scratching or soothing cream offered relief. It was as though an untamed energy had merged with the blood pumping through her body, begging to be free.

Thoughts of the woman's message haunted her daily, leaving her with a constant sense of unease. Maddie slept at night in quick bursts, awakening to those words humming in her ears.

Welcome to the Sisterhood. A gift is waiting for you when you are ready to claim it.

Unable to grasp its meaning, she struggled to imagine what the gift could be. Perhaps the lighthouse keeper knew more than she realized. She needed to go back to Neptune Point and speak to the man.

"I know that faraway look, Maddie Harlow. Big birthday plans tomorrow?" Nellie emerged from the living room as she sashayed into the kitchen. Grabbing a spatula, she set to work placing the cooling pastries into a plastic container. "I packed the tins of cookies in the trunk and started the car. It's freezing out, my window is frosted over."

"Winter's sneaky like that," Maddie said.

"So are birthdays." Nellie soaked a cloth in soapy water and wiped the counter. As she draped the cloth on the oven towel rack, her arm tattoos of vines weaving through a skull alongside roses appeared animated.

It had been almost a year since Nellie stopped by Maddie's market table. She had been twenty-four—nearly ten years younger than Maddie—fresh out of culinary school, raising a child, working at a local restaurant, and had dreams of starting a business of her own someday. What started as a partnership at the local market and celebration cake orders eventually grew into a trusted friendship. Nellie's talent for creating pastries and cakes resembling art, and Maddie's business savvy, was sending them on the path to open their dream bakery, away from the confines of a crowded market stall.

The Tough Cookie, just like us.

Tucking loose hair back into her braid, Maddie approached a large cheesecake resting on the island counter Aiden had built for extra baking space. "Thanks, Nell, but I've got everything I need, no big plans required." She gently shook the pan, and the center of the cake jiggled. "This is ready for the fridge. I'll top it up with cherries in the morning."

"Are you sure? I'll call some friends to come out dancing or we could grab dinner at the Casting Spoon tomorrow night. Zach can stay home with Jess."

"I'm sure, but you're sweet," Maddie said as her mind drifted to Aiden's gray skin as he laid in her arms the night at Neptune Point. He'd been fine ever since, despite her begging him to see a doctor for the cause of his 'fainting spell'. It was all she could think about.

She needed to go back and talk to the lighthouse keeper. If she was quick, tomorrow she could pack up and escape the market as soon as it closed for the afternoon, returning home before Aiden and Gabe's birthday plans. She'd simply knock on the lighthouse keeper's door and introduce herself. What was the worst thing that could happen? Perhaps a fool's errand that turned up nothing, but she had to try.

"Well, at least let me take Gabe for the night." Nellie glanced at her reflection in the kitchen window above the table, feathering her bangs. She tucked her short hair behind her ears and faced Maddie. "He had fun last week when he stayed over, and your night away was a bust—"

"I can't ask you to do that—"

"You're not, I'm offering."

"He'll want to do the birthday thing with us, he loves that stuff." With Aiden's family in Ireland, and her parents gone, evenings alone had been rare until Nellie had come along, and she'd gotten used to not relying on any help.

"Easy, I'll come get him after dinner, and he can watch a movie with Jess before bed. The bunk beds are perfect, he loves them, and Jess thinks he's hilarious."

"Hilarious?"

Nellie gathered her pastry supplies from the drying rack and put them in a vinyl bag. "He's got Aiden's charm, Maddie, look out."

"Okay, if he wants to go, I'll take you up on the offer." Maddie gave Nellie a quick squeeze.

"Oh no, get back here." Nellie hugged Maddie, taking her breath away. "When Miss-never-hugs gives a hug, I hug back. Hard."

"I hug... I do!" A breathless laugh escaped through her pursed lips.

"Aiden and Gabe maybe, but that's it." Nellie released her and grabbed her coat from the back of the chair.

Maddie followed her to the entryway, stopping to add a log to the fire. With a sharp crack, the dried bark gave way, sending a shower of sparks as the flames erupted. "Go home to your little girl and I'll see you at the market first thing in the morning."

A smile crossed Nellie's face, and her eyes sparkled. "I never knew a love like this existed. I love her more than my entire life, I'd die for that child."

Headlights cut through the darkness, rounding the turn as Aiden's truck rumbled up the long driveway. Gabe bounded out of the truck, holding a square box as the engine turned off. "I know that feeling." Maddie sighed as she stepped onto the porch, hugging herself as the evening chill seeped through her loose knit sweater to her skin.

Nellie hurried to her car, zipping her coat and shoving her hands in thick mittens. With the engine idling, the frost on the windshield had thawed, and she tossed her purse into the car, hopped in, and waved as she drove off.

"I'm going to work on those ships someday, maybe I'll build one or something." Gabe's red hair stood on end as he tore his hat off and strolled past his mom into the house, still carrying the box as he disappeared into the kitchen.

Raising an eyebrow, she narrowed her gaze at Aiden as he carried a duffel bag up the porch steps. A life spent on fishing boats had become part of their normal, but it was the last thing she wanted for their son. Gabe idolized his father and if she let him, he'd spend all his time in the dockyard with Aiden instead of school. The dread that gripped her every time a storm crept in while Aiden was gone for days or weeks at a time left her sick with worry. At least lobster season kept him close to home, but that was coming to an end. If anything happened to him and she wasn't around to help him the way she'd done last week… She blinked repeatedly to keep tears from welling in her eyes and shake the dark thoughts from her mind.

His weathered face beamed as he set the bag on the porch swing, easing the anxiety creeping into her overthinking mind. He loved his life, and she loved him even more.

Her pursed lips relaxed, breaking into a smile that mirrored his playful expression. "Did you go to the competition for that cake?"

Wrapping an arm around her waist, Aiden pulled her close. "Absolutely not, Nellie did her thing, but it's supposed to be a secret," he murmured before kissing her.

Her arms fell away from her tight grip on herself, and her hands slid up his back, embracing him. "I hug people, right? Am I not a… *hugger*?" She gripped the thick material of his coat.

Laughing, he leaned his head back. "Unless it's Gabe or me, not really, love. Why are random strangers trying to hug you?" Grabbing his bag off the swing, he kissed her forehead and headed inside the house. Gabe called out from the kitchen, bombarding him with questions about lobster traps and boat engines. Aiden kicked off his boots and hung his heavy coat on a hook in the entryway. He made his way through the living room toward the kitchen as he responded to Gabe.

They're home, safe.

With a deep exhale, Maddie shoved the front door, but it resisted with a scraping sound against the tile. An oddly shaped rock wedged at the bottom kept the door from closing. As she crouched to pick up the stone, a cloud of mist, like a cluster of a thousand tiny icicles, swirled up the porch steps. Loose strands of her hair whipped against her cheeks as the cloud of ice loomed in front of her. Heat radiated from her palms, enveloping the stone. Her skin burned along her fingers where the stone touched, and as she held it at eye level, a grating voice like scraping metal brushed her ear.

"Never safe here." The words hissed like escaping steam before fading into a high-pitched whistle.

Maddie glanced over her shoulder, but Aiden and Gabe were still in the kitchen, their voices muffled by a buzzing dominating her ears. The taste of metal filled her mouth as she fought to steady her shallow breaths, a lump in her throat tightening with each ragged gasp. She had never wanted to cross the hedge separating life and death, nor did she desire the rare gift. Seeing the dead was not a *gift*. She'd fought hard for life where the other side could never touch her.

A sudden brush of sharp bristles stung the side of her face. Flinching, she touched her cheek, and the stone fell from her fingers, striking the floor. She recoiled as a sticky substance clung to her fingertips.

Blood.

A wave of acrid smoke, the same as the night at Haven, hit her as the dark mist retreated into the night air. She slammed the door shut and leaned her back against it.

Aiden peered around the opening connecting the kitchen and living room. "We heated up leftovers, I'm starving." He stepped toward her, extending his hand to her cheek. "You're bleeding, what happened?"

Ignoring the paralyzing fear sinking into her bones, she moved around him and quickly snatched tissues from a decorative box on the coffee table. "I was fixing my hair and my ring scratched my cheek." She twisted the silver band adorned with a crowned heart on her ring finger. This ring was smooth, without sharp edges.

Aiden's concerned gaze followed her as she spun around and dashed toward the kitchen to escape further questions. Had whatever darkness lurking outside followed her from Neptune Point? "You made food, you say?" she called over her shoulder.

Since moving to this town, the lighthouse at Neptune Point had a relentless pull on her, like a physical tether in her chest. The weight of her mystical heritage steeped in an unseen power she knew little about had always made her feel like an outsider until she found a sense of belonging here. But this recent wave of strange magic and darkness sent terror through her for the first time in her life, and she wouldn't rest until she figured out how to absolve herself from its chokehold.

Three

Maddie 1985

With a jarring thud and a protesting groan from her aging car, Maddie gripped the wheel tighter as she navigated over a bump. The road curved, and she slowed to cross the bridge toward Neptune Point. The sun had disappeared below the horizon and darkness enveloped the sky. Clusters of stars emerged around the moon, but their combined light couldn't compete with the powerful beam of the lighthouse.

She parked and got out, tying the belt of her coat tighter. Sweat pricked her palms despite the cold air blowing from the sea, and she rubbed her hands on her jeans. Seagulls dipped over the cliffs, swooping over the roof of the house at the bottom of the hill, but the incessant waves crashing against the rocks drowned out their cries. Movement from inside the house cast a shadow through the window, illuminated by a single porch light.

He's harmless. Just an old guy taking care of an even older lighthouse.

She slid the cuff of her sleeve up, exposing a watch secured to her wrist with a simple leather strap. Although it appeared to be midnight, it was just after five o'clock.

Straightening her back, she shook her sleeve back over her icy hands and rummaged for a pair of gloves stuck in the canvas bag draped across her body. As she descended the hill toward the house, the shadow moved inside again. The lighthouse beacon's steady rotations shone through the curling smoke billowing from the chimney. The sweet aroma from the wood burning within the large house mingled with the sea's brine and seaweed, and if she shut her eyes, she could be standing at the end of her own driveway, inhaling Jupiter Cove Beach. Instead, she was at Neptune Point, debating on how to introduce herself to Aurora's keeper.

Nearing the front porch, she traced her fingers along the streaks of peeling paint and retrieved a fallen baluster, placing it against the railing. The boards groaned underneath her boots with each calculated step up the few stairs leading to the front door. Raising a clenched hand to knock on the door, her mind raced with how she would greet the mysterious man who lived here.

Hi, I'm Madeline Harlow... nice to meet you... I believe you have a gift for me... what in the hell is going on out here?

She breathed in the salty air, attempting to release the tension knotted in her stomach. Stretching her neck from side to side, she knocked once, but something rustled among a fenced plot of dying crops. Curiosity propelled her closer to the edge of the porch. Glowing eyes glared at her as she held the railing with both hands, leaning over. A raccoon darted from the bushes, scurrying under a torn part of the fence, and she jumped back, gripping her chest. She had just taken a deep breath when a deep, raspy voice startled her.

"There's nothing left. Either died with the frost or critters got to them before they ever had a chance."

Turning, she locked eyes with the lighthouse keeper. Lines stretched across his face like an engraved map of age, but a storm of wisdom and calm filled his penetrating gaze as he held the door open.

Warmth from a blazing fireplace collided with the icy air as he stepped onto the porch. "You returned," he said.

She swallowed and cleared her throat. "I heard... I thought..." Her rehearsed words dissolved in her mind. Not only would this man not be able to help her, but he'd think she was talking nonsense the moment she breathed a word of the strangeness going on around her.

"Mmhmm. Aren't the first, won't be the last." He observed her with an unblinking stare, and she looked away, shifting her focus to the garden of weeds as he continued. "Tea?"

Her head snapped back to him. "I'm sorry, what?"

"You drink tea? It was my favorite part of nighttime until my wife died. Now, I drink it alone. I don't even like the stuff, but it reminds me of her."

His thin frame slumped as he adjusted the suspenders holding up his trousers before smoothing unruly strands of white hair. A nervous flutter in her chest battled with ingrained caution about entering a stranger's home, and she'd almost forgotten why she was standing on his porch. But his despair was palpable, like an oppressive ache, and she couldn't find it in herself to refuse a cup of tea with him. "I drink tea."

"All right then." He held the door open with a gesture of his hand for her to enter. "You're not from here—your accent, I mean."

"Navan... north of Dublin." Her gaze darted from the open door, falling on flames dancing in the fireplace of a stone hearth in the living room, and back to the man wavering as he held the door for her. "Over ten years ago now."

"The boy yours?" The man stepped over the threshold, pausing just inside the open doorway.

He must've seen her coming to Neptune Point with Aiden and Gabe when they'd camped at Haven. "My son's ten, and yes. The man's mine too... my husband, I mean. He'll be looking for me if I'm gone too long." The words tumbled out of her mouth before she could stop them.

He's harmless.

Maybe he knew secrets about this secluded place and the lighthouse... *Aurora*, that could help her make sense of the impossible.

"You coming inside?" His thick, white eyebrows furrowed above intense eyes. "I just got that fire going pretty good, but the heat won't stick around with the door hanging open."

Like an icy finger, a shiver tore through her, and she folded her arms across her chest. She should at least know this man's name before sitting down for tea in his house. "Who are you?"

He extended a bony hand toward her. "Name's Jack Morana. Forgive my poor manners."

The handshake surprised her with its warmth, traveling through her gloves to her chilled skin. "Madeline Harlow, but everyone calls me Maddie."

"Maddie." Releasing her hand, he turned his back to her and muttered unintelligible words as he crossed the living room and bent down near the fireplace.

Casting a quick glance over her shoulder at the top of the hill where her car waited, she shut the door and trailed behind him. Curtains hung over a sofa against the wall beneath the window, obscuring the porch light. Shifting closer, she examined a stack of books propping up a leg of the oval coffee table in the center of the room. Her cheeks flushed from the heat of the fire as she strained to read the titles in the flickering firelight.

"History books, but I already read them, and I haven't gotten around to fixing that table," Jack said. The flames crawled along an oak log he tossed into the fire, casting shadows on the walls. "I'll go make that tea." He didn't wait for her, leaving her standing alone as he shuffled into the kitchen.

A grand room opened off the living room with a winding staircase leading upward. The wooden floorboards creaked under her feet as she wandered toward a piano commanding attention from the far corner. She envisioned dinner parties with people gathered around this room, captivated, while someone played beautiful music. The faint scent of varnish and a large dining table surrounded by six worn chairs hinted at a past where this house had bustled with life.

Removing her gloves, she tucked them into her pocket and lifted the dusty piano cover. Her fingers brushed the ivory keys, sending a cascade of delicate notes floating above the clatter of dishes and running water coming from the kitchen.

Jack appeared in the doorway from the kitchen. "You play?"

"No, but I wish I could. Do you?" Though still guarded, her fear had diminished, replaced with curiosity. She'd bet Aiden's most expensive bottle of whiskey that these walls held stories sad enough to shatter a heart of stone.

"My wife did." His eyes watered as he stared at the piano.

"I'm sorry, I shouldn't have—" Maddie lowered the lid onto the keys, careful to not let it strike against the wood.

He raised his hand. "Don't be." His gaze drifted up the stair-case and a smile cracked his weathered face. "She likes hearing it play again."

Maddie lifted her head and peered in the direction he was looking, but the landing at the top of the narrow steps was empty. "There's no one there."

"There's always someone here, Maddie," he said, his eyes fixed on the landing at the top of the stairs.

Teatime promised to be interesting.

Four

Maddie 1985

Jack gestured for Maddie to follow him into the kitchen. As they passed by a door hanging on its hinges, he shoved it closed, but a gap remained and she peered inside. Beyond the broken door, a wooden staircase descended into a dark, musty-smelling basement. Could the secrets of this place lurk down there?

He crossed the kitchen and pulled out one of the mis-matched chairs around the table. "Please, sit."

She shrugged her coat off and hung it on the back of the chair as she took a seat. A high-pitched whistle cut through the room and steam charged from a teapot on the stove. Her hand flew to her mouth, silencing a startled gasp as Jack stumbled while maneuvering toward the cluttered counter and extin-guishing the burner's small blue flame. The situation should terrify her—sitting in the home of a man who believed his dead wife was upstairs, but a sense of unnerving stillness surround-ed him.

Dropping a tea bag in each mug, he poured water from the teapot, its intricate floral pattern a stark contrast to the dimly lit room. He offered her milk as he placed the full mugs on the table, but she declined and swirled the tea bag in her cup with a gentle stir. "Your home is really lovely."

A chuckle escaped him as he sat across from her. "It's home. It'll always be home." He reached across the table for a pipe and stuck the end in his mouth, striking a match. Holding the flame over the opening of the pipe, he took a few shallow puffs, sending smoke billowing around him. He swiped at it with his hand as he observed her. "Does smoke bother you? No one ever comes here, and I didn't think to ask."

"I don't mind," she said. The tea burned her lips, and she flinched, placing the mug back down. The smoke stung her eyes, and she resisted the urge to brush it away, forcing a neutral facial expression.

Smoke curled from his lips, making him squint as it drifted over his face. "You sure? Your face is red." A wave of toasted spice and leather rolled off the pipe smoke, much different from the bitter smell of Aiden's cigarettes, and oddly comforting. But smoking was the one habit Aiden had that drove her mad with worry.

"You got me, I lied, I do mind. I make my husband go outside when he smokes, I wish he'd quit. But this isn't my house and I won't be here much longer." She took a deep breath and coughed, mentally scolding herself for lashing out at the man sitting across from her. "I have a reason for coming here tonight."

Jack picked up a brass tool that resembled a nail and stuck it in the bowl of the pipe before setting it on the ashtray. "My apologies, consider it out." He sat back in the chair, his hands clasped around his suspenders. "What is it that brought you my way, Maddie Harlow?"

She tapped her fingers on the table, pausing over a blemish in the dark wood as she contemplated the best way to ask him about the woman and the mysterious gift. Perhaps he didn't believe the dead stayed... *dead*. Not if he thought his wife was still in the house. A shiver crawled up her back, settling at the base of her neck. "What was your wife's name?"

He sipped his tea, observing her. "Lila," he rasped, his voice like the friction of sandpaper on wood.

Maddie curled her fingers into a fist, her nails digging into her palm as she ignored the tightness in her chest, hinting at fear's stubborn persistence. "You think she's still here... in this house?"

He stopped smiling, his pleasant demeanor replaced by an unsettling stare. "She's the reason you're in this house."

He knows something.

Her frantic heartbeat drummed in her ears, and it felt as though she'd swallowed cotton, but Maddie cleared her throat and pressed on. "How is that possible? I never knew your wife."

"You didn't have to know her to be connected to this place." He shrugged, releasing his suspenders as his hands fell to his sides.

"This place is cursed."

"Cursed? There's no curse." He ran a hand through his wild hair and leaned forward with his elbows on the table. "You're drawn here because of who you are, it's got nothing to do with any curse."

"But the locals—"

"Don't understand a goddam thing. They don't see past their own noses." With a laugh, he slapped the table.

Maddie grabbed her coat off the back of the chair and stuck her arms in, pulling it tight across her body. "What do you see that they don't then? Care to share?" Anger rose from her chest, sending a flush of heat to her face.

His face resumed its stoic composure. "I see none of it but know it's there… Its messages." He touched his ear. "It's a voice sometimes. It isn't something I can explain, shouldn't have to, really. Not to someone like you. Why don't you tell me what you see? We'll start there."

She rummaged in her coat pocket to grip her keys, letting the cool metal soothe her nerves like a security blanket. "I was camping with my husband a few nights ago at Haven—"

"I saw you. I always see you."

"Do you know how creepy that sounds?" Maddie rose, yanking her keys from her pocket. "I'm sorry." She ran a hand across her face. She'd made a mistake coming to see this man. His nonsensical ramblings and strange comments only caused a growing sense of dread. "I have to go, thanks for the tea."

As she walked by him, he seized her arm, releasing her when she glared at him. He stood and faced her with a heavy exhale, but she turned away, rushing to the door.

"Don't leave, I didn't mean to scare you," he pleaded as his eyes widened. "I know you don't trust me, but you need my help. I won't hurt you, you have my word. I made a promise to her, and I'll forever keep it, in this life and the next."

"What are you talking about?" Maddie spun around as a log snapped in the fireplace, sending sparks into the air. The embers landed on the surrounding stone and turned from orange to ash.

Jack took a few steps toward her. "She wants me to give you something. Told me she's been waiting for you."

"Who, Jack? Your dead wife?" A burning sensation pricked the palms of her hands, and she held them up.

"The lighthouse bears her grandmother's name, *Aurora*. And you've got the same magic she had." He approached with his gaze fixed on her hands.

"You know?"

"I don't get out much, don't really talk to anyone, not really." With a slow nod, he lifted his head toward the winding staircase. "But she talks to me, hell, I've got no one else. I saw you the other night. Saw the flowers. I heard her talk to you... You heard her too, didn't you."

The serene aura that had surrounded him outside returned and enveloped her with a sense of *knowing*. He meant her no harm, and she had to listen. "Aye, I heard her whisper to me," she said.

"You're ready then?"

No, never, I'll never be ready. I just want a normal life without any of this.

But a fierce need to know what he had to show her burned in her chest, holding those words inside. "I'm ready."

He ambled across the empty dining room to the bottom of the staircase and gripped the railing as he ascended the stairs. Maddie moved the living room curtains aside and surveyed the yard, suppressing the impulse to run back to her car.

Pausing on the staircase, he looked over his shoulder. "You coming?"

Deafening silence filled the room, interrupted by the crackling fire. "Maybe I'll just wait here for you to bring it downstairs."

"Suit yourself, but no one's up there, except..."

"Except who?" Leaving the safety of the door behind, she approached the bottom of the stairs.

"I help them if I can, but when they get lost, I'm not who they need."

A shadow streaked past the landing at the top of the stairs, and a sudden chill crawled over her skin. She fastened the buttons on her coat. Her breath caught in her throat, but she followed him up the stairs.

I must find out what he knows.

Jack flicked a light switch on the wall in the hallway, banishing the shadows. He opened a door at the end of the hall, letting icy air escape from a large bedroom. A sensation of fingers brushing along her cheek startled her, and her skin was cold when she touched it. An unsteady breath released from somewhere beside her. Hugging herself, she trailed Jack into the bedroom.

"Is your wife here with us now? I hear someone." Maddie choked on her words and coughed as the acrid stench of burning flesh returned with a vengeance.

Another light came on inside the bedroom, and Jack opened a closet door. "Do you believe in witches, Maddie?"

"Maybe." Of course she did. She was one. "Yes, I do."

"That's what I thought." Using a large metal key, Jack unlocked a closet, but when he opened it and pulled a rope dangling from a light bulb on the ceiling, narrow wooden stairs lead further up. He turned to face Maddie, the glow of the light making him appear angelic. "You see, it isn't my wife who I talk to in this house. No. She's gone."

Maddie gulped. "Who then?"

"Her grandmother, Aurora. I've got something for you."

With each passing moment, the enchantment of receiving a special gift faded, replaced with suffocating dread.

FIVE

MADDIE 1985

Jack abandoned the closet and rummaged through a mess of tools and combs in the dresser drawer beside it. He picked up a flashlight and turned it on and off, and back on with a grunt. "This'll do." His feet scuffed along the floor as he entered the closet and glanced over his shoulder. "You coming? The stairs are narrow, but sturdy enough."

Palpable darkness beyond the first few steps led up to an unknown room. Maddie's need to know what was happening to her battled with a frantic need to charge out of the room and escape the house, but once again, her curiosity held her in place. "I'll just wait here."

"Suit yourself." He disappeared into the closet, and his heavy footsteps echoed over the creaking steps.

A frigid draft snaked through the upstairs, colder than any night spent camping in a tent, and Maddie stood shivering near the ornate four-poster bed. Blankets covered the bed in a chaotic mess, presumably to keep Jack from freezing to death—how could he sleep in this cold?

Rubbing her hands together, she wandered around the room, pausing in front of an oval mirror resting atop a dresser. She lifted the tarnished lid off a tin box, revealing an assortment of earrings and necklaces. Running her fingers over a pair of diamond earrings placed side by side, her gaze fell on a photo of a woman with long dark hair with a child snuggled in her arms.

Lila?

Maddie moved closer to examine a gold locket against the woman's throat, but as she put the earrings back in the box, a pocket watch nestled beneath intertwined necklaces caught her eye. With a delicate touch, she traced her fingers over the etched lines on the gold case.

Footsteps shattered the silence above her head, jolting her, and she closed the lid on the box. The man had gone from living an entire life in this house with a wife and children to communicating with a dead woman in a lonely existence of emptiness.

She shuddered and moved closer to the window. Floral printed curtains with an overlay of yellow-stained lace hung on a crooked rod. On one side, the curtain's hem draped over a nearby table, burying a potted plant. Maddie probed the dry, cracked soil, trying to coax the wilted leaves to show signs of life, but the plant was beyond saving.

"You just need a little water and some love," she whispered.

A blast of icy air enveloped her in a smoky haze, and she spun around as a tornado of purple light swirled in the mirror. Brittle leaves crumbled in her fingers as she stepped closer and reached a hand toward the strange light.

Am I losing my mind?

The whispers of a woman, close and insistent, buzzed in her ears like a swarm of bees. "Try again."

"Try what again?"

"Breathe life."

Maddie spun around. "Like I did to Aiden? Are you the reason he's alive?"

The strange purple light spilled from the mirror and surrounded the plant in a shimmering haze, rustling the leaves.

Maddie rushed to the window and flung the curtains aside, but the window was closed tightly.

The tingling sensation returned to her hands, and she scratched them, lifting her palms to her face. A faint, lavender glow pulsated from their centers, accompanied by a wave of warmth that spread along her skin like a gentle caress. The magic surged through her, a tempestuous hurricane of power that battered against her ribs, leaving her breathless.

"Breathe. *Life*." The woman's breathy whisper brushed against Maddie's ear again.

As Maddie touched the dying plant's leaves, a subtle pull from inside her chest sent a current of electricity down her arms. Vibrant green enveloped the brown leaves, causing them to unfurl and expand. The soil dampened under her fingertips, and with a last burst of light, flowers bloomed. Jumping back, Maddie tripped on a pair of tattered slippers and gripped the post of the bed to keep from falling. The amethyst smoke in the mirror swirled and shifted, forming words.

Embrace light.

With gasping breaths, she stepped closer to the mirror, her heart pounding. Her hand trembled as she let her fingers brush the mirror's surface, torn between fleeing the house or obeying the message and meeting Jack upstairs. What was taking him so long? A heavy silence hung in the air, thick and suffocating. The mist escaped the confines of the mirror and curled around her fingers, clinging like an icy grip. Fear should've forced Maddie to yank her hand away, but a calm presence surrounded her instead as the words faded, vanishing into a puff of purple haze.

The closet door slammed shut, and she spun around, gripping the dresser. The ceiling moaned, and thuds resounded above her head as dust billowed down to the floor.

Maddie bolted to the closet and flung the door open as Jack's muffled, desperate voice filtered through the ceiling. "Are you okay up there?" She called up the stairs inside the closet, but he didn't respond.

She ascended the first two steps with a knot forming in her stomach. "Mr. Morana? Jack?" As she slowly climbed the dark stairwell, an eerie silence greeted her. She never expected to spend this much time in a strange house with even stranger things happening. Aiden would be beside himself with worry, not knowing where she was.

Light cascaded down from above and Jack's shadow emerged at the top of the stairs. "I took a fall, but I'll survive another day." He held up a large book. "I found it, but she hid it well. Too well. Come up if you want, I'll show you around. You need to know this house in case…"

The stairs creaked under Maddie's feet as she made her way up into an attic, not taking her eyes off Jack's silhouette at the top. "In case what, Jack?"

He handed her the flashlight as she approached him at the top. "Hold this," he said.

The weight of the handle in her grip empowered her, offering the potential of a weapon should she need one.

"Sure is cold up here, cold everywhere lately." Jack adjusted the book in both hands and placed it on top of a rustic trunk.

Moonlight glinted on intricate cobwebs strung like silver threads from a round window to the wall. "What did you find? What's the book in your hands for?" Every breath she took fogged in front of her, and she wrapped her arms around herself as she crept around the attic.

"For you." He tapped the book.

Shining the flashlight on the book cover, Maddie ran her fingers along the image of a faded hand with an intricate eye at the palm's center. "What am I supposed to do with this?"

"I'm just the messenger, she wants this in your hands, not mine. First time I ever saw it."

She angled the flashlight toward Jack; the beam catching the flecks of gold in his eyes, making them sparkle. "*This* is the gift. I came out here for a book?"

He chuckled and rubbed the back of his neck. "Nothing is just anything around here, you can trust me on that. Open it, start there."

She peeled back the cover of the leather-bound book, revealing a detailed drawing on the inside page. The shadow of a man glared back at her from the depths of a forest, his crimson eyes like burning coals, brighter than the fire depicted in the background.

Never safe here.

The words whispered at the edges of her mind. Resisting the temptation to turn the page, she held the flashlight closer. Swirling lines resembled a river churning between the trees... *Haven.*

"Who's the man in the picture?" she whispered.

"She tried, really tried." Jack scuffed along the floor near the top of the staircase. "Take it with you, she needs your help... They all do." A burst of mist expelled from his mouth as he exhaled in the cold. "My work here is done for now." He headed back down the stairs, not waiting for her to follow.

She stood still, staring at the image on the inside cover of the book. "But I don't understand." The pages were blank as she flipped through the rest of the book. "A book with no words?" The frigid air in the attic chilled through her skin. She yearned for home where she could soak in a bath with water so hot it burned her numb skin.

"Come down from there and out of the cold, Maddie," Jack's voice called from below.

Snapping the book shut, she hurried down the rickety steps back into the bedroom. He pulled the rope, shutting off the lightbulb, and locked the door behind them. "What am I supposed to do with this, Jack? Who needs my help, anyway? The dead lighthouse woman? What does she want? You can't just leave me with this"—she held the book up with both hands—"and not tell me what it's for."

A smile returned to his face, and he patted her hand, gripping the book. "You'll figure it out. They always do."

"Who?" She trailed him through the hallway and back down the winding staircase. "No offence but I didn't expect a cup of tea with a lonely man to turn into a haunted bedroom with purple mirror messages, magic plants, a book with no words, and you've got nothing to say about any of it?"

He meandered to the fireplace, grabbing an iron poker as he stuck a log in and brought the flames back to roaring life. "No offense taken."

"That's what you got from what I just said?"

"I'm not as lonely as you think, Madeline Harlow."

"I'm sorry, I was rude. It just came out a jumbled mess."

"Usually does under the circumstances." He plopped onto a chair near the fire. The orange flames cast shadows in the living room.

"Right... *circumstances.*" She held the book against her chest. "So, speaking of my unusual circumstances. You seem to know more than I do, any advice? Will what happened upstairs keep happening to me?"

The chair rocked as he leaned back, letting his head rest on the cushion. "I'm just the messenger."

She inched toward the door, the weight of the book settling in her arms. "That's it? You gave me this book; told me she wanted me to have it. Come on, give me something, anything!"

The chair stopped rocking, and he stilled. "My wife died in this house. We had a long life together, raised a family." Jack gripped the armrests, his eyes brimming with tears.

Guilt sank into Maddie's chest for pressing him. In his peculiar way, he was trying to help, and she'd have to figure the rest out on her own. "I'm sorry, Jack, I've stayed long enough. My son and husband will be waiting—"

"It was her grandmother who allowed her to leave... *really* leave, ya know?"

Not exactly.

"The same woman who helped me save my husband?" Maddie leaned against the door, her feet shifting on the wooden floor. Anticipation for his next words coiled between them like pressure building in a bottle about to shatter, spilling a truth she wasn't ready to hear.

"The same indeed... Aurora. It's impossible to keep your power a secret, and the dark one will come for you regardless, I'm afraid." He wiped his eyes. "She's going to help you get rid of him again, Maddie. She'll always come." His brows knitted together as he observed her.

"What dark one? Is that who's been following me, telling me I'm not safe?" Fear was winning. Jack's unsettling knowledge of her secret life as a witch with magic wouldn't offer the help she needed, not if someone dark on the other side had discovered her powers and wanted to hurt her. "Was your wife—was Lila a witch too?"

"No. Aurora took it away, made sure magic didn't touch her daughters or their children in case anyone found out. But Lila knew who her grandmother was, no matter how hard her mom tried to keep the truth from her." Jack pushed his foot against the worn wooden floor, the chair creaking in protest as he rocked it again, his gaze falling away from Maddie. "Lila's mother was ashamed, thought it to be a dreadful curse, you know? Always told her she thought witches were supposed to be evil, and it damn near broke Lila's heart." Lifting his head, his eyes met Maddie's, a spark of recognition passing between them. "She knew there'd be others, and there are, especially in this town. There's a pull here, moths to a flame. It's the river, the sea, it's the magic surrounding her lighthouse."

A slow exhale escaped Maddie's lips as she released the pent-up air in her lungs. As Jack revealed the truth, the unspoken pressure hanging between them dissolved. Leaving the security of the door behind, Maddie stepped into the room, placing the book on the table as she sat in a chair across from Jack. "And here I am, one of the others."

"Here you are indeed," he said.

"We agree on one thing, Jack."

"What's that?"

"Witches aren't the evil ones, quite the opposite." Maddie guarded her mystical secret, not from shame or embarrassment, but to avoid the lingering centuries-old judgment. The light magic, a constant, gentle thrum, had been with her since she was a child, its soft, golden energy like a second heartbeat pumping life through her. And the magic had saved her husband.

Breathe life.

"I'm real happy you stopped by this evening," Jack said. "I suspect your journey is just getting started."

"It would appear so." She rose from the chair and picked up the book from the table. "Any last words before I go?"

He chuckled with a sigh. "She won't be far, I assure you. Especially not now that her book found you, but there's nothing more I can do." Standing, he stretched, smoothing his wild hair on the sides of his head as he moved toward the door. "I'll see you out, then."

Maddie stepped onto the front porch as he held the door open. A blast of icy wind whipped across her face, stealing her breath and making her eyes water. "Thank you, I think. I don't know what else to say." In her soon to be thirty-three years, she'd never had a night quite like this one.

"Don't be a stranger," Jack said. "Next time you come out here, I mean."

She nodded, clutching the worn book to her chest as she descended the creaking porch steps.

The door shut behind her, the echo lost to the waves against the rocky shore, only to open again. "Maddie?"

With a hesitant breath, she stopped and turned to face him. "Yeah?"

"What you lose, will find you again one day. Look for the glimmers, got it?"

"No, Jack, I don't get it."

"You will." He retreated into the house, leaving her alone and freezing in a state of confusion as his shadow disappeared behind the living room curtains.

A dark silhouette moved through the trees near the entrance to Haven, mirroring the illustration in her book. Her skin crawled with a terrifying premonition and the words *never safe here* repeated in her mind. Fueled by adrenaline, she raced uphill to her car.

Blasting the heat and the radio, she escaped Neptune Point, her breaths coming in ragged gasps. But as she crossed the Bifrost bridge onto the road toward home, the book on the passenger seat pulsed with a vibrant purple light. Aurora had a message for her, and she had no choice but to pay attention.

Six

Maddie 1985

Maddie arrived home and ambled past Aiden's truck in the driveway toward the front porch. Her footsteps crunched on the frost-covered lawn, and the echo of waves along the shore carried across the road, not as thunderous as the rocky shore of Neptune Point. As she walked up the porch stairs, she held the book out in front of her.

She couldn't tell Aiden, he wouldn't understand. He simply believed he'd married a woman who had a deep affection for nature and gardens. Secrets of the dead, and magic that brought life back to the dying, were better left unsaid—and she had no plans to reveal them. Not to anyone.

As she tucked the book underneath her arm, the door swung open. "Happy birthday, love." The orange glow from candles on the mantel and flames dancing in the fireplace made Aiden's red hair redder, and his green eyes sparkled. From behind his back, he presented a bouquet of flowers wrapped in butterfly paper tied with a fuchsia ribbon.

Warmth surrounded her as she stepped inside, and Aiden shut the door. "What's the book you got under your arm?" he asked.

"It's nothing." She smiled and placed the book down next to her bag on the floor. The glowing light had stopped, but she folded her coat and gloves on top of it, concealing the cover and any magic that might seep through. "Let me see those luscious beauties." Taking the armful of flowers from him, she inhaled the rose-scented powdery aroma and beamed. "How do you know exactly what I need?" Tucking the flowers against her, she reached for his face and brought him close to her, planting her lips against his. "Where's Gabe?"

"You're late, Mom." Gabe rushed across the room to embrace her. With his recent growth spurt, he was transforming with each passing year. She didn't think she'd ever be ready for her little boy to become a grown-up and leave home behind. "I'm going to Nellie's tonight but I got you a present, come see." With one last squeeze, he ran back into the kitchen, almost tripping over the brick surrounding the fireplace.

"Careful!" Maddie's throat tightened as she yelled.

"He's okay." Aiden's hand found the small of her back as he followed her into the kitchen.

"It smells like home in here." She lifted the lid from the pot on the stove and waved the comforting aroma of sweet and savory Irish stew toward her nose. The satisfied expressions on Aiden and Gabe's faces melted away the fear and worry from earlier, like a safety net wrapped around her.

"We cooked." Aiden picked up a ladle and stirred, scooping potatoes, carrots, and beef into the spoon. "I even used a bottle of Guinness—not the same as home, but better than nothing."

"Never the same as home," Maddie whispered.

"This is home," Gabe said, handing her a small box wrapped awkwardly with pink paper and tied with a lopsided ribbon. "I like our house."

Ruffling his red hair, Maddie took the gift from him. "What's this?"

"Nope, not telling, you got to open it."

Maddie unraveled the ribbon and opened the package, trying not to tear the paper.

"It's just paper, rip it open." Gabe's mischievous expression was a mirror image of his father. They shared similar features with their green eyes and freckled cheeks.

With a grimace, she ripped the paper off and opened a square box. A crystal butterfly, the most stunning shade of royal blue, lay nestled in tissue paper. With delicate fingers, she picked it up, examining the trinket more closely. Tiny flowers formed an intricate pattern along the open wings, and its sapphire body gleamed under the overhead light.

"I don't know what to say, darlin'. This is... it's everything." She blinked back tears, bowing her head to keep them hidden from his view.

"He saved up his earnings helping me over the summer, bought it himself." Aiden beamed at Gabe, the pride between them tangible like an overwhelming tidal wave of adoration.

Her family was her lifeblood, and the gift her son gave her would always symbolize their bond in a way she couldn't comprehend.

Aiden spooned stew into three bowls and carried them to the table as Gabe plopped into his usual chair near the den. "You love the butterflies in the garden when they change from a caterpillar into something pretty, and Dad and me found this at a cool store in town."

"On the corner with the turquoise flower boxes under the windows?" she called out as she carried the butterfly into the living room and placed it carefully on the mantel.

"My friend Anna told me her mom said it's gonna close so it's a good thing we got it," Gabe continued from the kitchen as she stepped back, admiring the crystal figurine.

A subtle lavender glow emitted from underneath her coat in the entryway, and she rushed to bury the book deeper, tossing a scarf over it.

Aiden peeked around the corner of the living room. "Are you hungry, Mads?"

"Starving, but you already had me at flowers and the best gift a girl could ask for." She forced a smile to cut through her nerves and left the book behind to join them at the kitchen table, shoving the haunting thoughts of Jack, Aurora and Neptune Point away from the edges of her mind as fear's ache threatened to consume her.

Maddie sat across from Gabe as Aiden handed her a glass of red wine, poured how she liked it, almost touching the rim of the glass. As she sipped the maroon liquid, an inner warmth spread through her. "You have a new friend?"

"I told you, Anna."

"Is she new in town?" Maddie blew on a spoonful of stew as she eyed Gabe.

Aiden grabbed a beer from the fridge and used a multi-tool set from his pocket to pop open the bottle cap as he sat back down. "Her mom's Theodora Tate, they live in those fancy houses across town."

"Marble Gate Estates?" Maddie asked.

"That's the one." Aiden locked eyes with Maddie, sharing a look filled with unspoken understanding.

Lifelong town locals, who'd raised generations and never left, had a reputation for their lack of hospitality.

Gabe stopped eating, his gaze darting between his parents. "She's nice, I like her. I might be able to go to her house soon, can I go if her mom says it's okay?"

Please don't get caught up in their world.

Maddie smiled at her son. "I think that'll be all right, tell Anna to have her mom call me."

"I'll write our number down for her, and also, her parents have a boat." Gabe glanced at his father. "Maybe you could get a boat of your own, too." His eyes widened as he settled back in his chair. "Then when I grow up, I'll learn how to take care of the boat stuff, you know, fix it when it breaks, help you catch fish—"

"How about you worry about school first, like homework, reading, math." Aiden took a long drink of his beer.

Gabe made a face. "How about we have cake instead?"

"You're in a hurry," Aiden said between bites.

"Nellie's coming with Jess after dinner's over, I can't wait." Gabe eyed the clock on the wall. "What time is it?"

Nellie was right. He loved it over there. Maddie rushed a few more bites before answering him. "It's six o'clock, and they'll be here at six thirty." She tilted Gabe's bowl, finding it empty. "Want to go ahead and just have cake now?"

"Yes, please." Gabe dragged a wooden stool along the tiled floor close to the island counter.

Aiden produced a lighter, the flame dancing as he ignited the silver-coated candles on a cake adorned with such life-like fondant flowers, dragonflies, and butterflies that they appeared to take flight, leaving an intoxicating sweet vanilla aroma behind.

"Nellie's so good." Maddie gasped. "It's pure art."

"You'd kill me if I got a cake from anyone else." Aiden smirked.

"Never," she said.

The image of him sprawled on the cold, damp ground, his chest heaving as he gasped for air, face contorted in agony, flashed through her mind. The thought of losing him that night filled her with a profound and agonizing dread. Keeping her teary eyes averted from his, she rotated the glass dish, examining the frosted details of lilies, cherry blossoms, and lotus flowers. She paused, captivated by the white roses set against the intricate greenery.

A dull ache spread from her chest, tightening its grip along her jawline as memories of her teenage years working with her mother at a flower shop in Ireland flooded back.

White roses are for funerals.

The chilling loss of her parents in a car accident when she was twenty had reshaped her life, changing her perspective forever. Her mother's voice had been the first whispers from the other side, opening a locked door to magic she'd never believed existed. Aiden's unwavering support when she'd met him one year later, had become a lifeline as she navigated a new life on her own.

"Make a wish." Gabe's voice shattered her thoughts, bringing her back from her painful recollection.

"A wish..." She shrugged. "I don't know what I could wish for. I've got everything I need inside this house."

"There's always something to wish for." Leaning forward, Aiden rested his elbows on the island countertop.

"Not always, but here goes." Closing her eyes, she let her mind wander to what a future in this house looked like, but a barrier like a thick, black curtain fell, and fear coursed through a feeling of emptiness. The evening with Jack and the strange book crept into her mind.

I wish for this place to be our safe haven forever.

She blew out the candles, extinguishing the flames into thin wisps of smoke.

The smell of melting wax filled the kitchen as Aiden pulled the candles from the cake. "That looked pretty serious."

"Nothing too serious." Maddie handed him a cake server, and he cut three equal pieces, presenting the first plate to her like it was a crown.

She took a bite, savoring the perfect balance of sugar and chocolate in the middle, licking the sweet frosting off her fork.

Aiden studied her face with furrowed brows. "Your wishes will come true, I know it."

"I hope so." She placed her palm against his cheek, and he kissed her hand.

Headlights beamed through the living room window, and Gabe scraped his plate clean, hopping off the stool as he bounded out of the kitchen.

Aiden sat on the bed, leaning forward with his elbows on his knees as Maddie stood staring out their bedroom window. Her fingers grew numb as she clutched the curtains closed, leaving a gap between the edges. The branches on trees around the yard swayed, and a streetlamp across the desolate road cast a lonely glow on the rocky cliff side, but all appeared normal—whatever that meant anymore.

"Where are you tonight?" Aiden asked.

She yanked the curtains closed and sat beside him on the bed. "Here with you."

"Could've fooled me." He unbuttoned his shirt and lay back on the bed, tucking his hands behind his head.

Curling up next to him, she draped her arm across his bare chest. Aiden was her safe place, her person. He was her home and she couldn't imagine a life without this man by her side. "I'm here, I promise. It's you and me like always." She trailed kisses along his neck and he rubbed her back.

"There she is." He wrapped both arms around her and placed a kiss on her forehead.

She lifted her head and cupped his face in her hands, meeting his gaze in the dimly lit room. "Let's block the world out tonight, okay?"

"It's your birthday, whatever you want, love. This is just the beginning," he said as his hand reached behind her head, guiding her face closer to his.

"If this is the beginning, I can't wait to see how it all ends," she whispered.

"I hope you never have to." A serious expression settled on his face, and a slight frown etched itself onto his lips. "I love you, Mads. More than life, I swear."

"I love you, too." She pulled him closer, and his arms tightened around her as he swept her beneath him, enveloping her body with his, their mouths meeting in a heated, desperate kiss.

She traced her fingers down his back as his hands slipped underneath the hem of her shirt, warming her skin and relaxing the tension in her body. His shallow breaths matched her own, and his lips moved along her jawline. He pulled back, his gaze lingering on hers, seeing her like no one in the world could. She brushed unruly strands out of his eyes. She'd memorized every line on his face as though his familiar expression held a private language just for her, communicating without a single word spoken.

He blocked the world out, and in this room, in this moment of intimacy, as the rhythm of their breaths filled the quiet between them, they weren't simply Madeline and Aiden Harlow. They were soulmates who had found one another; lovers who'd created a beautiful family, embraced in a love so profound it took her breath away.

Time ceased to exist, and when exhaustion claimed them, she collapsed underneath the covers, falling asleep in Aiden's arms.

Maddie 1985

Chimes radiated like a broken music box in Maddie's head. The faint ringing intensified into a persistent, metallic clang that vibrated from her pillow inside her ears. As she bolted upright in bed with sweat trickling down her back, the sound halted, plunging the room back into silence except for Aiden's gentle snores. The antique clock had captivated her every week for months at the market until she'd bought it a year ago, and this was the first time its chimes had ever made a sound. But rather than a melodic lullaby, the echo of metal reminded her of warning bells.

The cotton sheets clung to her skin as she swung her legs over the side of the bed. She grabbed Aiden's over-sized shirt, buttoning it up as she made her way downstairs. Only embers remained in the fire, and a chill in the air sent goosebumps over her skin. As she rushed toward the den, icy fingers wrapped around her arm and she spun around, gasping.

"Is someone here?" she whispered as she touched her cheek. Had the dark force returned? Could it get inside?

An amethyst glow bathed the entryway, and she crouched down, pushing her coat off the book. She turned the pages, each one without a single word, and flipped back to the inside cover. The dark silhouette appeared to move through the trees, lifting a cloaked head as faint light illuminated two eyes. Snapping the book shut, she sat on the floor, clutching it to her chest as a harsh reality crashed into her. The secrets hidden inside the strange book included her, and if she was going to keep her family safe, she had to uncover how she fit in with this new world.

The book's light spilled over the floor, sending heat along her fingers as she carried it through the kitchen toward the den. With the second hand on the clock in the kitchen inching past three in the morning, the standing clock in the den had stilled at exactly 11:11. The pendulum that had caused chimes to ring moments ago now stood motionless, creating an unsettling silence.

She placed the book on the desk, allowing the light to illuminate the room, and rapped on the glass face with her knuckles. With gentle hands, she explored the polished wood, the scent of aged varnish faint beneath her fingers as she followed the carved vines and flowers to the butterfly-shaped corners at the top. She strained as she shoved the clock, but it wouldn't budge away from the wall, searching for a simple explanation but found none.

Maddie sat at the desk and restlessly stacked a cluttered mess of receipts and invoices for wedding cake sales, her gaze shifting between the clock and the book. Tapping her fingers on the leather-bound cover, she slid the chair closer.

What am I supposed to do with you?

Frigid air swirled from out of nowhere and lifted the cover, slamming the leather against the desk. The impact mimicked the frantic drum of her heart against her ribs, pulsating into her bones, and she flung herself against the back of the chair.

"No, you don't get to scare me, not in my own home." A strangled gasp escaped her lips as she spoke, her words catching in her throat. But knowing the dead walked among the living differed from witnessing their power in action. Days before her mother's death, she'd told Maddie something that had haunted her ever since.

"Only the very gifted can see them, hear them, feel them. Stay on your toes, Madeline, and you might be fortunate enough to glimpse past the hidden veil to the other side someday."

Maddie had dismissed her mother's tales of folklore and fairy trees as delusional ramblings. It had never occurred to her that her mother had clung to a knowing of her own. A sudden high-pitched buzzing filled her ears, and she covered them as it escalated and stopped. As she dropped her hands to the desk, a woman's voice replaced the silence, and Maddie bolted upright, listening as she tried to make out the woman's words. The scent of burning hair and skin assaulted her senses, and she stood, gripping the edge of the desk.

The pages fanned quicker than her eyes could keep up with. Ribbons of purple light curled along the spine of the book, lifting off the pages and drifting out of the den into the kitchen. She grabbed the book and treaded along the cold floor, following the light as it surrounded the vase of flowers resting on the counter. As the shimmering light hovered over Aiden's gift, the rose buds unfurled, their crimson petals bursting open.

Consumed by fascination, Maddie moved closer, the weight of the book heavy in her sweaty hands. She'd never seen anything like this before, never felt like this before. A tingling current pulsed beneath her skin with each shallow breath and heat radiated from the palms of her hands to her fingertips, but what startled her most was the sense of calm washing over her like a steady rush of warm water.

"Your turn." The woman's whispering became clearer, and the words hummed like a haunted lullaby, mesmerizing her like a hypnotic spell. "Embrace your gift, Madeline."

"How do you know me?" Setting the open book on the counter, Maddie touched the soft rose petals. Three more scarlet rosebuds, their velvety petals furled, were nestled in the heart of the bouquet. Fading purple light streamed from the book, and although she stood alone in the kitchen, a mystical presence surrounded her. "I gather you're not the dark one Jack told me about who paid me a visit the other night."

The whispers quieted, and the dancing light stopped moving, leaving an unnerving stillness in the room.

"I'll take that as a no," Maddie said. Goosebumps erupted on her skin, and she rubbed her arms, tucking Aiden's long sleeves into her palms with her fingers. "If you just tell me who you are, what you want, what I'm supposed to do with this magical book, basically anything at all, I'd appreciate it. I'd like to move on with my life—"

"Aurora. Madeline, you are in danger." The voice spoke louder with a new assertiveness, sending the light bursting into a cloud of confetti sparkles that landed on the counter before disappearing.

As sure as she knew Aiden loved her more than life, Maddie could feel the ghost's intentions in her gut with an unwavering calm, and this dead woman—Aurora, wouldn't hurt her. The energy in the room crackled with a palpable, silent force like the eye of a hurricane, fueling her with an unseen strength. "So, tell me, Aurora," she breathed, her voice barely a whisper. "How do I keep myself and my family safe from something I can't even see coming?"

"Magic." Aurora's voice echoed in Maddie's ears as icy fingers curled around her wrist, dragging along her hand to her fingers.

Shivering, Maddie rubbed her chilled skin as an insistent pressure guided her hand toward the flowers. Her legs trembled, but she held herself steady, letting Aurora take the lead. The pages in the book blurred in a rapid flutter before settling on an empty page.

"The roses will respond to your magic as you breathe life." Aurora's whisper carried a promise to Maddie's ears.

Maddie touched the small rosebuds, gently holding each one in her fingers. "Nothing's happening." A purple mist swirled around the flowers as she exhaled, heat emanating from her palms, and she remembered the carpet of lilies at the Keeper's house. A jolt of electricity shot through her fingertips, and layer by layer, the petals opened until the red flowers flourished in the center of the vase. In a burst of fluttering wings, a butterfly emerged, flying erratically before landing on Maddie's fingers. Tiny veins pulsed with a faint rhythm as she traced the shades of blue in its wings.

Lifting her hand, she examined the peculiar insect, its tiny black eyes reflecting a distorted image of herself—an older woman, etched with lines around her eyes and forehead. A vision shattered the image with a flash of red hair, reminiscent of Gabe and Aiden's, and she gasped as the joyful laughter of a child sang in her mind.

With a delicate flutter, the butterfly danced above her head, leaving a mist trailing behind it before disappearing into a shower of glitter.

A sudden, crushing ache settled in Maddie's chest, and her stomach plummeted like a stone; the same feeling she got when worry consumed her, but this was different. A darker sense of unease weighed on her. "Aurora? Are you still here? What's going to happen to me?"

The sharp burning scent from earlier subsided into a sweet aroma of hickory smoke from a campfire as Aurora spoke close to Maddie's ear, her words articulated and slow. "I belong to the Sisterhood, as do you, as will she."

"You mean witches, don't you," Maddie whispered into the void, her eyes fixed on the book as fancy purple lettering crawled across the blank page, the ink bleeding into the cream paper, but the bright light obscured the script. "Who was that child laughing?"

"Mystics, healers, keepers of the light." Aurora's soft voice read each one aloud. "What once belonged to me shall belong to you, it is the only way."

The icy air warmed, caressing Maddie's face. She touched her cheek. The magic surrounding her transformed the kitchen into an ethereal world, stealing her breath.

Maddie gripped the counter as cursive script trailed across the pages of the book. "I just, I don't understand—"

"The dead are not the only ones wandering, Madeline."

The kitchen plunged into darkness, falling back into silence, except for the ticking clock coming from the den. Maddie rushed through the door to find the clock working once again. She stood staring at it without seeing it; the encounter with Aurora had left her with more questions than answers. Left with a strange vision of the future and a magical book that could write by itself from a long-dead witch...

The book!

She flicked the light switch over the island counter and read the words in front of her, tapping the rough pages as she ran her fingers over the shiny purple message.

Essence of night

Where the water flows,

The peak of the moon's power
Calling upon the ones who burned,
Vanquish harm through reflection.
Lock the door.
Seeking Haven for all, after and before.

It resembled a spell, like the ones she'd used with candles and sage to protect her home from negative energy, the only part of her magic that she'd ever let Aiden witness. He'd plant a kiss on her forehead, and mutter an endearing, "that's my wife", as he moved along.

Her mother's words echoed in her mind, but instead of seeing the dead, Maddie's power to revive the dead had extended from flowers to people. And now she was cursed with figuring out a mystery future involving a child she'd never met. The hair was too long to belong to her son, and the laughter didn't either. This was a younger child, someone else, but who?

The sudden weight of responsibility threatened to drown her as though someone dropped her in the middle of the ocean without a life preserver. The floor creaked above her, and she closed the book. The longer she played with magic, the more she risked attracting Aiden's attention and his questions, which she would never be able to answer. She brought the book of spells—or whatever it was—into the den and shoved it into the bottom desk drawer. Forcing herself to take a few deep breaths to calm her racing heart, she climbed the stairs back to bed.

"Everything all right?" Aiden greeted her as she entered the room. "I heard something downstairs."

"I couldn't sleep." Her gaze drifted to the opening between the curtains as light from the moon shone into the bedroom. A primal sense of danger washed over her, sending a prickling sensation on the back of her neck with a warning she didn't understand.

Aiden lay back on the bed and flipped the covers open. "Come here," he said.

She crawled in, letting him wrap his arms around her and feeling his warm breath against her head.

"Better?" His voice rasped, heavy with sleep.

"Better." She clung to his arms, holding him against her.

A comforting warmth spread through her as Aiden held her. As she clung to his arms, his breathing evened out into soft snores.

She would take care of whatever haunted her, and everything would return to normal.

It had to.

MADDIE 1985

Winter arrived early, blanketing Atlas Cliffs with a thick layer of snow. Maddie arrived home from the market and lugged empty containers from the car, battling powerful gusts of wind rolling off the ocean and over the cliffs. Opening the door, she stomped snow off her boots on the porch and dropped the containers on the entryway floor. The blizzard whipped a dark mist across the front yard with a chilling howl as it moved closer to the porch.

It's back.

Her hands burned, radiating an eerie glow under the surface of her skin, trembling as she lifted them up toward the dark cloud hovering near the driveway. "Leave now!"

A silent flurry of snow dusted the entryway floor as she gripped the open door. She stepped onto the porch, kicking the row of protective crystals she'd placed along the threshold.

"I said *leave!*"

The mist halted, inching closer as its edges blurred, disappearing into a cloud of smoke. The dark energy haunting her had refused to stay away, and the encounters had intensified over the past month since Aurora had gifted her the book. Crystals and protective spells from the book were no longer enough to ignore it, but she wasn't sure what she could use as a more permanent solution.

She rearranged the scattered crystals in the planter next to the door and hid a few more underneath a loose floorboard, reaffirming the words of protection. At least the spell prevented whatever terror lurked outside from entering her home.

As she shut the door, locking it behind her, a stillness surrounded her, eerie rather than welcoming. She removed her boots and hung up her coat, but a damp chill sank into her bones, offering no comfort. Aiden had prepared for the first storm of the winter and the metal box on the brick hearth sat filled with wood. He'd be home with Gabe for dinner soon, and her family would be together, safe.

Kneeling in front of the fireplace, she arranged kindling and crumpled newspaper before striking a long match. Tiny flames climbed higher, intermingling as they devoured the paper and crept along the kindling. A shower of orange sparks crackled as she added a large bark-covered log and replaced the metal screen. She stood, extending her hands toward the roaring fire and inhaling the sweet scent of wood smoke as its warmth chased away the winter chill.

Home.

On her way into the kitchen, she tugged on the metal chain dangling from a stained-glass lamp, casting a bright glow in the darkening living room. She took a lasagna out of the fridge covered with foil, glancing at the clock as she turned on the oven. It was later than she thought. Aiden and Gabe should have been home from the dockyard by now. Despite her protests, and with a pleading Gabe, Aiden took their son with him to finish up tasks on the boat before the storm, reassuring her they wouldn't be long. As the minutes ticked by, a growing unease clawed at her.

A blast of hot air escaped the oven as Maddie opened the door and swiftly placed the pan inside, shutting the door to contain the heat. The kitchen window above the table rattled as ice rain pelted the glass. A throbbing ache crawled from the back of her neck, spreading along the sides of her head. The unsettling premonition of something terrible about to happen clung to her like a shroud. She wished there was a way to reach Aiden, hear his voice, know they were on their way home.

A metallic clang echoed as the chimes struck from the den, and Maddie's throat tightened. Tears blurred her vision as she stepped into the dark room, afraid to look at the clock as each toll of the pendulum hammered against her chest.

The second hand continued its steady motion around the clock's face and the chimes ended as the time showed one minute past six o'clock. Aiden had promised her he would be home no later than five.

A thread of purple light reflected on the clock's shiny surface, vanishing as she ran her fingers over it.

"My heart hurts for you, Madeline." Aurora's voice trembled; a fragile whisper choked with unshed tears. "What you lose will come back again."

"What happened?" Tears escaped, trickling down Maddie's cheeks as the jarring ring of the doorbell sliced through the suffocating silence. Before her conscious mind could register what her heart already knew, a premonition of disaster clamped around her chest, squeezing the air from her lungs, leaving her numb as she hurried through the living room and flung the front door open.

Two police officers stood on the porch as a blizzard swirled around them in a chaotic blur. "Mrs. Harlow, I'm afraid we have some bad news." The shorter man took off his hat and gripped it in his gloved hands. "Your husband was brought to Silver Boulder hospital—"

"Is he okay? Our son was with him, Gabe, are they all right?" She fumbled with her coat, stuffing her arms in and zipping it up to her neck. With her purse over her shoulder and keys in hand, she braced herself against the wall, fighting to stand upright as her entire body shook.

The police officer cleared his throat before he spoke with careful hesitation. "Ma'am, Gabe is being treated for minor injuries, but I'm afraid Mr. Harlow is in critical condition. We'd like to offer to drive you, especially given the weather—"

"I'm ready, yes please, let's go." She wiped the tears off her cheeks as she shoved her feet into her boots.

He has to be all right, I can't lose him. I can fix him, if I get to him in time...

An emergency room nurse escorted Maddie to a hospital room, gently explaining how Aiden fell, crushed between the boat and the equipment he'd been using. In his room, a woman wearing green scrubs and a stethoscope around her neck eyed a monitor screen as it beeped in a slow rhythm. Thin tubes snaked from bags of clear fluid into Aiden's arms. Bright red saturated the sheets and blankets covering his body. Maddie rushed to his side, the chill of his skin a shock against her own as she took his cold hands, her lips pressing a fleeting kiss to each finger.

The woman observed Maddie with furrowed brows. "Your husband sustained fatal injuries, Mrs. Harlow. We're doing our best to make sure he's comfortable. I'm so sorry, there's not much time. Your son is in another room with a nurse, but he's all right—"

"Can't you operate on him? Put him back together?" Maddie choked through her tears and hyperventilating breaths. Life without Aiden was no life. She'd die, she'd curl up in a ball and die.

I can't lose him, I just can't.

A crushing wave of agonizing grief slammed into Maddie. This couldn't be real, couldn't be happening to her. She breathed through the pain in her chest, summoning magic to wrap around him, leaning over him and placing her hands on his bleeding body.

Breathe life.

"Please don't leave me," she begged him, squeezing his hands and his arms. "Open your eyes, Aiden. I need you so much, I don't want to do this without you, please, *please.*"

Maddie gasped for air, tears streaming down her face, her chest heaving with each ragged breath as she begged for Aurora to help her save him. "Help me! Where are you?"

His hand rose to her face, and he brushed his fingers against her skin as his eyes slowly opened. A glimmer of life reflected in his eyes, fading as his shallow breaths rattled in his throat. A pained smile stretched his lips thin as he clasped her hands. "You can do this, love. You will, for you and for Gabe."

"No, I can't. Not without you, never without you. It's supposed to be us forever, remember?"

"It will be, just not here. I'll wait for you wherever I go, love."

She pulled her hands from his as her palms tingled with a burst of magic, dulling into an icy chill. With a sharp inhale, Aiden took his last breath.

I'm too late.

Maddie came undone, sobbing, throwing herself over him, her fingers digging into his shirt as she clung to him, refusing to let go.

The beeping of the monitor ceased into a flatline, and the doctor turned off the machine, dabbing her eyes.

Maddie's world crumbled, a landslide she wished would bury her. But as she walked out of the room, with Aiden's blood clinging to her coat, and an unrepairable hole in her soul,

Gabe came running toward her, his face as red as his hair, and his eyes swollen with tears.

Overwhelmed with grief, he dropped to the floor, wailing as he sobbed, and Maddie gathered their son into her arms.

NINE

MADDIE 1985

Somehow, she made it through Aiden's funeral, battling her own despair to comfort her shattered son.

Friends, locals, and those who adored her husband had brought food, flowers, and hugged her with words of condolence as they gathered around her living room and kitchen. Like a hollow shell, she'd gone through the motions, but her mind was numb. A piece of her soul had been stolen, and not a sliver of hope remained.

As she sat in his favorite chair, her fingers absently trailed over the worn fabric on the armrests. She could almost feel his arms around her again.

I'll never hold him, smell him, hear his voice whisper, 'I love you', again.

Her head fell back against the cushion, and she glanced out the window, catching sight of Aiden's truck that the police had returned to her the day he'd died. It now sat covered in a layer of snow and ice with his belongings still inside. Fresh tears erupted, and she wiped her eyes with a crumpled tissue, trying to stop them from falling.

A sudden wave of gut-wrenching sorrow swept over her like an unseen hand, ripping the threads of her existence apart, and she rose from the chair, desperate for an escape.

Leaving Gabe with Nellie, Maddie fled upstairs, seeking refuge in the bathroom. She gripped the vanity counter so hard her fingers paled. Her swollen, red eyes stared back in the mirror with a vacant, unrecognizable gaze, and the emptiness in her chest threatened to hold her captive forever. She was ready to let it suffocate her.

A sudden spark prickled along her hands, and warmth spread up her arms, settling into her chest. Rubbing her hands against her pants, she turned on the tap and held them under cold water. "You were supposed to keep me safe, my family safe. Where were you when I needed you?"

A knock at the door echoed and water sprayed over her shirt as her hands flew to her mouth.

"Mom?" Gabe's voice came through the door muffled and hesitant.

She turned off the tap and dried her hands. Wiping her eyes, she took a deep breath and opened the door. "Yeah?"

Sniffling, he wiped his nose with his dress shirt sleeve. "People are asking where you went, I think they're going home now."

"I'll be right there, darlin'."

"That's what I told them." He chewed his lower lip, averting his gaze. "I don't know if we're gonna be okay anymore, with Dad gone." A tear trailed down his freckled cheek, and he used his damp sleeve to catch it. "I'm just too sad." His breath hitched through tears.

She didn't think her heart could break any more, but the hopeless look etched on her son's face sent a wave of agonizing pain through her. With slumped shoulders, he turned and scuffed his feet along the floor toward the stairs.

She rushed after him, summoning what little resilience she had left. "Gabe."

He wept, covering his face with his hands, and she embraced him, wrapping her arms around him. "I'm sad too, so damn sad." She cried into his hair, her voice a muffled whisper.

Leaning back, she pried his fingers away from his face. "Look at me." His shoulders shook uncontrollably, and she held his tear-streaked face in her hands. "You and me, we're going to be just fine, okay? I promise you. Whatever you need, I'm here." She forced a smile. "Remember what your dad always says?"

"Harlows are tough," Gabe said.

"You got it, we're strong, we can get through anything."

"It's too hard, Mom."

He spoke with wisdom beyond his ten years, and she searched for hope to give him. "That's why we look for the glimmers to keep us going until there's so many of them, we feel joy again."

He yawned, rubbing his eyes, but his lower lip trembled as tears erupted over his flushed cheeks.

"You want to get PJs on, and I'll say goodbye to our company?"

With a nod, he squeezed her in a bone-crushing hug, and she kissed the top of his head. She leaned against the banister as he ran into his bedroom and turned the light on.

I can't quit on us.

Maddie sat at the kitchen table holding a glass of red wine as her eyes drifted into a blank stare. The absence of Aiden's laughter and his familiar chatter amplified the emptiness inside of her. This place had never felt less like home.

"Gabe's asleep, dishes are done... Are you sure you don't want me to stay over tonight?" Nellie sat beside Maddie.

A hazy fog clung to Maddie's senses, so heavy it trapped her inside a bubble of disbelief. How could this be her life?

"Maddie?" Nellie put her hand on Maddie's arm.

Shaking herself from her somber trance, Maddie sipped her wine, barely tasting it. "No. No, I'll try to get some sleep."

"You don't have to do this alone. I know you well enough that you'll lock yourself away and try, but I won't let you." The neck of Nellie's sweater shifted, getting caught in her necklace as she folded her arms across her chest. "We're family and I'm going to be here for you like you've been for me."

Maddie swirled the deep red liquid in her glass, the image of a bleeding Aiden in his hospital bed flooding her mind and churning her stomach. She set the glass down and slid it out of her view. "I don't know how I'm supposed to do this—this, 'keep going thing'. What if I don't want to?"

Nellie's eyes welled with tears. "You lean on me, but you don't give up. Gabe needs you. I need you."

The constant ache pulsed from Maddie's chest into her neck, and she grabbed the glass off the table and tossed the liquid into the sink. The crimson dripped along the sides of the sink, trickling down the drain as she gripped the edge of the counter. "I want to scream."

"Then scream."

Choking back sobs, Maddie covered her mouth. "I'd terrify poor Gabe."

Nellie stood next to Maddie, putting an arm around her shoulders. "That's what the beach across the street is for, you can scare away the gulls."

"Right now, I scare myself, Nell."

"I know, but you're going to get through this. I don't know how, but you will." Nellie wrapped both arms around her, pulling her into a hug. Maddie surrendered, hugging her friend back, her shoulders slumping as she kept herself from collapsing to a pile on the floor.

"You sure you don't want me to stay?" Nellie said as she patted Maddie's back, releasing her.

"I'm sure. I'll survive." Grabbing a handful of tissues from a box on the counter, Maddie blew her nose.

"I'll come by tomorrow—" Nellie said.

"You don't have to do that, your life is busy enough—"

"I want to. I'll bring Jess and she can hang out with Gabe, keep his mind off things maybe." Nellie headed toward the door and put her coat on and gave Maddie one last hug. Maddie stood with the door open as Nellie drove away.

A crisp layer of frost covered Aiden's truck as it sat in the quiet stillness of the driveway, broken only by the steady surf of Jupiter Cove Beach across the road. Maddie slipped her feet into his worn leather boots and pulled on his heavy coat, inhaling his scent of tobacco smoke blended with leather and cologne as tears stung her eyes. An icy wind bit at her face as she trudged along the snowy pathway to his truck. Climbing in the driver's seat, she shut the door and gripped the steering wheel.

He had tucked his gloves in the center console beside an empty coffee cup. Gabe's untouched school bag sat on the passenger seat amongst discarded gum wrappers, a stark reminder of the day her life changed forever.

A vise squeezed her chest, making each inhale a desperate, shallow struggle for air. Her head throbbed with a dull, persistent ache, and every muscle in her body screamed in protest. How was she supposed to go on without him?

"Why me? Why us?" she yelled, her voice bouncing off the empty cab's leather seats and frozen windows.

With her hands curled around the steering wheel, a guttural scream ripped from her throat, shaking her whole body as she dissolved into uncontrollable sobs. Heat flushed her face, and her nose ran, leaving a trail of salty tears as she struggled to control her hyperventilating breaths. Slumping over the steering wheel, she let her head fall forward against her hands, surrendering into grief, and she cried until her head throbbed.

Her legs felt like cement blocks, and she couldn't bring herself to leave Aiden's truck. She couldn't put one foot in front of the other and move on. She couldn't breathe.

Bright lights shone on the driveway as a car pulled in, parking behind her. Tears blurred her vision as she adjusted the rearview mirror, straining to see who was in the car. The headlights of a truck older than Aiden's went dark, and a figure got out from the driver's side.

Who would show up here this late?

With Gabe alone in the house, fear and adrenaline coursed through her as her hand clutched the door handle, ready to get out and run to the front door.

TEN

MADDIE 1985

Knuckles rapped on the frosted truck window as Maddie opened the door, and the silhouette moved aside, giving her room as she stepped out of the truck. Wiping her eyes, she shut the door, retreating around the front of the truck as the porch light illuminated Jack's approaching form, his face etched with worry.

"I'm sorry for your loss, Madeline. I know that pain all too well." Jack removed his hat and held it against his chest as he spoke.

"What are you doing here? How did you know?"

"Word travels in this town." He placed his hat back on his head, the brim shading his eyes. "When I heard about what happened to him, I had to come, but I'll go if you don't want me here." His coat appeared to swallow his slight frame as he shoved his hands in the pockets and turned to leave.

An urge to stop him consumed her out of nowhere. "Wait," she said. Aiden's oversized boots thumped as she trailed behind Jack, and he stopped, facing her. "I guess I... I never thought of you as someone who came to town, and I haven't been to Neptune Point since that night, or I would've stopped in to check on you."

"I don't need checking in on. But a man's got to eat and get fuel, tools. I like the market sometimes. Your friend makes the best cupcakes, I don't get to have those much anymore."

"Nellie? You've been to the market?" Maddie wiped her face, letting her cold hands linger on her hot, tear-stained cheeks.

"Only a couple times, it's been a while," Jack said. "I suppose I should've said hello."

"Why didn't you?"

"Don't know." His gaze wandered over the house, drifting to the front yard. The soft glow from the porch light cast shadows over the sad lines around his eyes. "I just don't really know. I'm not too good at the social stuff."

Maddie let the sleeves on Aiden's jacket hang over her hands, curling her fingers around the soft leather. "This is his coat." She kicked her foot forward. "His boots."

"A little big for you but looks warm." His brows furrowed with a fatherly look of grave concern.

"It's all I've got left of him, you know?" Exhaustion settled into her bones, but another crushing brick of sorrow brought tears to her eyes again. "I don't think I'll ever stop crying."

Jack extended his hand and patted her arm, his touch feather-light on Aiden's jacket, conveying a silent understanding. "This isn't all you've got left of him."

"Gabe," she whispered.

"Your son's name?"

She nodded, tears streaming down her face, unable to utter a response.

Exhaling a sigh, Jack's breath curled in the night air. "It'll hurt less with time, but the pain will never go away completely. Just my experience." He let his hands drop to his sides and his coat sleeves draped to his fingertips. "I'd hug you if you thought it would help. I used to be pretty good at helping my kids feel better when they were sad, I'm just out of practice."

She'd never been one to hug someone as an automatic response to comfort other than her family, but loneliness hurt. "A hug would be great," she admitted.

Jack wrapped his arms around her and patted her back. He started to pull away, but she raised her arms and hugged him so tight she thought she might crush him.

Sniffling, she released him. Gentle snowflakes drifted from the dark sky and fell around them, melting into her hair and jacket. "Did you want to come in for tea or to warm up?"

He glanced at the streetlamp across the road. "I appreciate that, Madeline, but I didn't come for hospitality."

"I know, it's just freezing out here—"

"If you'll let me, I need to show you something before I go." With a sudden, ethereal look, his eyes flickered back to hers. "You need to know the truth and how to stop it from happening again."

She shivered, gripping Aiden's jacket under her chin. "What are you talking about?"

He lifted his unsteady hands toward her face, and she flinched, but a sudden flutter of the same presence that Aurora had brought into her kitchen enveloped her, relaxing her tense body. Heat radiated from his hands into her head like an electric current as a sharp taste of copper popped along her tongue. The energy surged into her chest, a warm rush that made her gasp, and a blinding vision forced her to close her eyes.

Gabe ran along the dock, stopping to look up at a crane as its cables swung, screeching under the strain of large equipment hanging from its grasp. A look of sheer terror filled Aiden's eyes as he ran up behind Gabe, yelling his son's name.

"What am I seeing? Is this..." Maddie swallowed hard, the lump in her throat feeling like a heavy stone as she fought back her constant flow of tears.

A dark mass swirled near the crane, forming the ominous silhouette of a cloaked figure with hidden features. A chilling stillness hung in the air as the horrifying spirit extended an ulcerated hand toward the metal object swaying from the ship over the dock. Aiden's panicked screams echoed as a piece broke off and tumbled toward the dock.

Like a helpless outsider, Maddie screamed, but it fell silent, reverberating through her mind. Aiden shoved Gabe out of the way as the chunk of metal pinned Aiden to the dock, snapping the wood with a deafening crack.

Jack's hands fell away as he stumbled backward, grabbing the hood of Aiden's truck for balance. "You needed to see for yourself," he rasped through rattling coughs. "I'm sorry, I didn't want you to know, but—"

"Why did you show me that?" She charged toward him with her fists clenched at her sides. "Tell me what that thing was, Jack! Is that what's been stalking me? Sneaking around my house? It wasn't after me? Why did no one tell me it was going to hurt my family, kill my husband!" She screamed until the air left her body, leaving her weak.

"I'm sorry, I didn't know." Jack exhaled, coughing again. "We thought the gate was closed, but he escaped." He stood, taking a step toward Maddie. "Aurora needs your help."

"My *help*? Where was she when Aiden was dying and I needed *her* help? Where was the powerful witch when this, this... *thing* came after my family!" Maddie paced back and forth, unable to catch her breath. "I want nothing to do with her. I'm done with this, with you. It's my fault he's dead. Because of what I am, I lost the only man I've ever loved." In a desperate, clumsy spin, she bolted for the porch stairs, but her foot slipped out of Aiden's boot, and she fell, landing in the snow. The ice melted, seeping through her pants, and she lay on the ground as the frigid cold numbed her legs until it hurt.

Snow crunched under his feet as Jack ambled next to her, extending his hand. "It's not your fault, it's mine."

"How in the hell is it your fault? I'll never forgive myself, not ever. He's dead because of me." Rejecting Jack's offered hand, she rose and thrust her wet foot into Aiden's boot. "It's over, I have to go inside and check on my son."

"I am afraid it is not yet over." This time it wasn't Jack who spoke, it was a woman.

Aurora.

"Leave me alone." Maddie waved her hand through the intensifying snowfall and grabbed the railing as she stood on the first step.

Aurora's voice carried over the rhythmic crashing surf in the distance, as though she were speaking into Maddie's ear. "Your husband saved your son's life, but the one who seeks your power will return until we banish him."

"So take it then!" A wave of prickly heat crawled along Maddie's palms as she lifted her hands. "He can have my power, I don't want it. Tell me, Jack, if I have so much power, why can't I see her?"

"I don't know. I can't hear or see her."

Maddie stepped back onto the ground toward him. "Then how does she communicate with you? How did you know to come here tonight and show me that... that disgusting—" Her hands flew to her mouth to stifle a cry. "This isn't real. It can't be real." She paced back and forth, muttering to herself.

Jack shook his head, the wrinkles between his brows deepening. "The mirrors. She sends messages in the mirrors. Sometimes I can hear her, but only near the lighthouse."

"How do we get rid of it—him, whatever that thing is?" Maddie whispered. "I will die to protect my son."

"He embodies wickedness, a hunter of witches who refuses to stay dead. He is not the first, and he will not be the last." Aurora's haunting words filled the space between Maddie and

Jack. "With the radiance of a full moon, a witch among the living, the Sisterhood among the dead, a spell from your book, and this."

A swirl of purple light crackled with energy and enveloped Jack, settling over his pocket. He lifted a silver chain with an obsidian pendant out of his pocket, letting the chain drape over his fingers as he handed it to Maddie.

"What's this?" She took the jewel from him. Vines crept along the surface of the crystal, their entanglement blocking out a glow of purple haze at the core. The jewel thrummed with electricity underneath Maddie's fingertips and the chain draped over her hand.

With an icy chill settling around her, the unseen ghost-witch said, "My amulet was not meant to fall into your hands until a different time had come to pass. Magic dwells within this pendant that can banish the dark ones who cause harm, and as long as you possess the jewel, the power of protection lies in your hands. Guard this talisman with your life, for it shall be required by others like us. Like *you*. Should its magic fall into his clutches again, her fate shall be sealed, she will die, and no one will be safe."

"Who is *she?*" With trembling hands, Maddie draped the necklace over her head and clutched the amulet close to her chest.

"Meet me in the forest where the river flows between the trees, where all things begin and end, on the eve of the full moon. I will ensure you are rewarded for the sacrifice you've endured." Aurora's voice thinned into a faint murmur, and her presence departed, leaving Maddie and Jack surrounded by falling snow.

Maddie's body protested, aching with every step as she stumbled inside the house. A shiver ran through her as she removed Aiden's coat and carefully draped it over the back of his chair in the living room. The pain of losing Aiden was too much. Life felt like a suffocating, relentless pressure threatening to consume her.

I can't do this without you.

She dragged her weary body upstairs into their bedroom. A pile of Aiden's T-shirts sat untouched on his dresser, and she traded her clinging wet clothes for one of his worn shirts and familiar sweatpants, tying the drawstring tightly around her waist.

Gabe's panicked yell sliced through the air, and fear gripped her stomach as she tore into his bedroom. "What's wrong?" She rushed to his side, wiping damp hair from his frightened eyes.

He sat up, throwing the blankets off himself. "I don't want to be in here alone, can I sleep in your bed?" He grabbed his pillow and headed for her bedroom as he talked. "It was a nightmare about a man who wants to hurt you, but I couldn't see who it was. I know it's a dream, but it felt real, Mom."

He crawled into her bed, and she slid in beside him, rubbing his back. She held her breath until her lungs burned, forcing her to release it. Jack was right. This wasn't over. "You're right, darlin'. It was just a horrible nightmare, no one will hurt us."

"I know. I think I just miss Dad so much I'm having bad dreams." Gabe's breathing settled as his tears slowed, and he trembled as he yawned.

Maddie's hand found the amulet in the darkness and its weight settled in her palm. She would meet Aurora on the night of the full moon and end this. Once and for all.

ELEVEN

MADDIE 1985

The moon appeared larger than life, outshining Aurora's towering beacon with its bright radiance, the snowy path to Haven gleaming under the silver light. The chimney of the Keeper's house puffed out a lazy plume of smoke, with only an orange glow hinting at a fire burning inside.

Aiden's coat kept Maddie warm as she stood under the canopy of low-hanging spruce tree branches. Her fingers encircled the amulet, and as she took slow steps forward, its heat seeped into her skin. The ache of guilt constricted her chest, each strangled breath a painful reminder of her role in Aiden's death. She'd lived a quiet life with a gentle herbal magic, never imagining that her abilities had marked her and her family as targets for something sinister.

Leaving Gabe with Nellie, she'd hidden an envelope containing her final wishes in the jewelry box on her dresser. She'd be damned to death before she let anything happen to her son. The crisp air whipped at her cheeks, and she pulled her knit hat over her ears as she trudged forward. As she approached Haven's clearing, the rushing current in the Coda River grew louder, and her boots sank into the deeper snow near the water's edge.

Movement among the trees caught her eye, and she surveyed the surrounding forest. "Aurora? I'm here. I'm ready." The amulet pulsed with violet light, its glow reflecting off the untouched snow. "Let's get this over with."

Maddie faced the river, captivated by the white-capped water as it churned too fast to freeze, dragging rocks and fallen branches toward the ocean. She stepped over a boulder, closer to where the water met the bank, and let the current tug on her boot. Her shallow breaths clouded in the frigid air. Was death the only way for her to see Aiden again? A part of her wanted to succumb to the river's pull and let the waves carry her away, never to return. But the image of Gabe's freckled face and beaming smile snapped her out of her numb state and back into the present.

A sudden screech like a train whistle shattered her concentration as she clambered back up the riverbank, but a brutal impact of something powerful and unseen knocked her off balance. With a startled cry, she lost her footing and slid over the icy rocks. Her arms and legs flailed as she fell toward the river, and the water soaked through her gloves, numbing her fingers as she grabbed at branches.

Warm hands enveloped hers and pulled her upward. Jack grunted as he supported himself against a rock. "Can you stand?"

She kicked her feet, bracing her boot in a patch of soft snow, and pushed herself up. He released her, and she climbed over the bank to safety, collapsing on a fallen log. "You came?"

"She said you needed help."

"Of course she did." Standing, Maddie brushed snow off her pants and stormed away from the river near the clearing where she and Aiden had camped for their last time. "If only she showed up when I really needed her." The rage inside her burned, defying the numbing cold that gripped her flesh.

"Madeline!" Jack called from behind her as a tornado of black mist swept up snow and encompassed her.

Fingers like sharp blades wrapped around her throat, clenching tighter. A strangled gasp escaped her lips as she clawed at her neck, and the world dissolved into an explosion of stars behind her closing eyelids.

"Help," she cried between shallow breaths.

A thick, suffocating darkness closed around her, plunging her into a cocoon of unnerving silence except for a voice scraping against her ears.

"Mine," he hissed.

The amulet tore away from her skin, leaving a burning trail as the feeling of icy shards of glass, sharp and unforgiving, cut along her neck. Magic spread like wildfire through her, both strange and familiar. The tingling sensation coiled underneath the surface of her skin and surged down her arms, settling in her hands like a presence that belonged there.

"We shall banish he who hunts us with a thousand deaths until we meet our own." Aurora's voice resonated in her mind as a flash of amethyst light sparkled around her. "You will never be alone, Madeline. They are all here, we are ready for you to send him back where he can not hurt another soul."

An instinctive knowing what she needed to do settled in her chest with a strange calm as Maddie reached for the amulet, tugging the silver chain from the entity's grasp. The jewel pulsed with shocking electricity in time with her heartbeat. A circular beam radiated from the amulet with a light so blinding it was as though the moon had collided with the sun, creating a portal.

Warmth cascaded from her head to her toes, and oxygen flowed back into her lungs as the pressure relieved from her throat. Out here, in the forest she'd once adored so much, she wasn't just Maddie. She was part of something bigger, something ancient and powerful, and surrounded with so much... *love.*

"Welcome to the Sisterhood, Madeline Harlow." Aurora stood beside her, and for the first time, Maddie could *see* her.

The woman stood in a haze of sparkling purple mist, the light catching the dark strands of her hair as they whipped around her head like a halo. Curls of smoke emitted off her gown as it billowed around her. Aurora stepped forward, closer to the swirling light, and layers of black fabric rustled over the snow. The lace-trimmed sleeves slipped down as she extended her hands, and reddened, burned flesh along her pale arms caught Maddie's eye.

"He murdered you, didn't he?" Maddie's breath caught in her throat as the churning smoke shifted into a cloaked man. A menacing growl rasped from him as his polished boots thundered closer, stopping inches away from Maddie.

Laughter escaped the spirt hovering over her. "You cannot win, I will hunt you, I will remove all those around you until none of your kind remain."

Tears pricked Maddie's eyes, blurring the world as her heart pounded against her ribs with a force that threatened to tear them apart. "I can't hold it back, Aurora."

Aurora tilted her head to the side and a gentle smile graced her lips. Her eyes sparkled with an ethereal light as she looked at Maddie. "As it should be." She glanced over her shoulder. "Jack?"

But Jack had already moved silently to Maddie's side, holding up an oval mirror that reflected a distorted image of the trees around them.

Aurora spoke the words that had appeared in the spell book, and other voices chimed in, joining her. Light projected from the amulet toward the dead man, dragging Maddie with it.

"Speak your intentions with clarity, Madeline. You tell the magic what you need, and it shall oblige. We are all here for you," Aurora urged. Her assertive voice echoed from everywhere and nowhere all at once.

"I want him to leave me and my family alone."

"Not to me, speak to him," Aurora demanded. As her smile widened, purple magic swirled and gathered in her palms.

With a sharp exhale, Maddie released a wave of warm magic, but the entity's fingers snaked toward her throat once more. She didn't back down, advancing forward until her eyes held his vacant stare. "A forever death isn't long enough for killing my husband." Maddie surrendered to the power coursing through. "I want you to *burn*." Tears streamed along her numb cheeks, leaving a burning trail. The spell had etched itself in her mind's eye and the words spilled out effortlessly. "Essence of night, where the water flows, the peak of the moon's power... calling upon the ones who burned."

Ghostly silhouettes emerged from the forest, surrounding her, and the door to the other world, the gate, shifted like floating water. The realm's light faded, and a wind dense with ice rain sent violent shivers through her body. "I can't do this anymore," Maddie's voice cracked.

"Yes, you can," Aurora's voice echoed from behind her. "Do it for Aiden, for Gabe, for your legacy to follow."

An electric buzzing filled Maddie's ears, forcing her to release the amulet and press her hands against the sides of her head. "I can't! Leave my son alone and take me, take what you want!" She crumpled to the ground, and the shadowy spectre lunged for her with an oppressive wave of darkness, surrounding her.

A sudden, heavy silence, cut off the buzzing, and a sliver of light broke through the cloud of death. "You're not dying tonight, love." Aiden's voice cut off the sinister force draining the life from her body as he crouched beside her.

"Am I dead?" She brushed her fingers along his forehead, letting them trace his familiar features. His skin was softer than she remembered, and his green eyes brighter—as though they had light of their own.

"You're very much alive, Mads." He scooped her up, setting her gently down with her feet on the ground. His gaze lifted to the ominous, dark mass of energy. "Do us a favor? Take care of that will you?"

"You can do this, I need you, Madeline," Aurora said, her magic holding the witch hunter's wrath away from Maddie.

"Don't leave me," Maddie cupped Aiden's face in her hands. "Please don't go, not yet."

"Wouldn't dream of it, not till you're safe, love."

Jack angled the mirror toward the diminishing light marking the gateway into another world. "I can't see what you can," he said. "I can only feel the vengeful anger hanging around you and it's not leaving."

Words of the next part of the spell flashed through her mind.

The mirror had a purpose.

"Hold that mirror up, Jack, get ready, this has to work." A stream of shimmering light stretched from the amulet as Maddie moved toward the cloaked dead man. "Vanquish harm through reflection." A flash struck the mirror, and Jack dug his feet deeper into the snow to steady himself as fragments of glass rained down over the snow like diamond dust. Maddie flinched but continued to recite the spell as a familiar energy of witches gathered around her. "Lock the door, seeking haven for all after and before."

The dead man's cloak flew open, unleashing a stream of fire that stole the air from her lungs. The intense heat scorched her skin like a sunburn, and she dropped to the ground. A final burst of light from the amulet engulfed the ghost of death, and a wretched scream tore from his distorted body as he disappeared inside the portal. The circular light imploded and collapsed, leaving behind a scattering of gray ashes blanketing the snow.

Breathing deeply to fill her lungs and steadying her racing heart, Maddie leaned against a tree for support. The gurgling rush of the Coda River's current broke the profound silence. The moon cast eerie shadows over Haven's clearing, but all mystic light had disappeared.

She grabbed the amulet, holding it up. Its heat subsided into a gentle warmth, and a streak of purple light flitted along the inside walls like a firefly before extinguishing into an onyx stillness.

"Aiden?" she shouted into the emptiness, the sound bouncing back from the riverbank as it echoed over the rushing river.

Jack approached with slumped shoulders. Deep lines of exhaustion etched his face, his eyes heavy-lidded and bloodshot as he looked at her with a weary gaze. "It's over," he said. He patted her arm and plodded onward through the snow along the path leading out of Haven.

"You're just leaving me here all alone with nothing?"

Pausing up ahead, Jack slowly turned around. "You're not alone Madeline, take a look around? If you can't see, *feel*." He lifted his hands with palms facing the sky and dropped them into the pockets of his long coat, whistling as he disappeared beyond the tree-lined path.

A fresh wave of energy crept through Maddie, weaker than before. Tingling, like a thousand tiny sparks, danced across her palms. The river glowed with a neon light, and Maddie pushed off from the rough bark of the tree, scattering pine needles as she hurried to the riverbank.

Lotus flowers covered every inch of the Coda River as far as she could see, blooming out of the water like beacons of light to drown out the darkness.

"I have not forgotten my promise," Aurora whispered.

"Please come back to me." Maddie fell to her knees, sinking into the snow, and picked up one of the vibrant flowers. As her fingers brushed the petals, threads of light spread through them.

"Hi, love." Aiden appeared next to her, taking the flower from her hands. He tucked it in her hair and moved strands off her face.

She threw her arms around him, burying her face against his chest, absorbing the warmth of his body against hers. He embraced her, tilting her face up to meet his gaze. "You didn't do this to me, stop blaming yourself. You're going to be okay, maybe not today, but one day. And you're needed here." He glanced past her face, and the angelic shimmer in his eyes was a painful reminder that this would be the last time she'd ever hold him again. "This won't end with you, Mads."

His jade eyes, flecked with gold, returned to hers, and his fingers curled in her hair, tugging gently as he brought her mouth to his. The kiss held reassurance that they were here together, deepening into a yearning as though her magic could intervene and keep him here, on the side of the living, until she was ready to join him.

His touch faded as their connection broke apart and his forehead rested against hers. "I love you, forever," he said, his voice barely audible.

"I love you forever." Tears pricked her eyes as her fingers intertwined with his, a gentle smile gracing her lips as she kissed each of his fingers.

He smiled, his touch lingering on her face one last time as he backed away and disappeared. The flowers sank like heavy stones, leaving behind a sweet fragrance as the river carried them out to sea.

Desperate, she reached behind her, searching for something—anything—to stop herself from sinking into the earth. She leaned against the uneven surface of a boulder with her palms against the cold, dampness. Gabe needed her, she had to keep breathing, keep moving forward, keep *living*.

Magic had both saved and cost her the love of her life.

A subtle purple glow settled beside her as Aurora's soft, haunting voice whispered in her ear. "You will no longer see but hold fast to your magic. Let the amulet be your companion and keep the book near."

A blissful warmth cascaded over Maddie's head, its gentle caress easing grief's dull ache as it clutched her chest. "Will you be back?"

"Only when the time comes to guide the wandering on their journey."

"The dead, you mean?" Maddie said, staring at the waning light next to her.

"The dead are not the only ones wandering, Madeline." Aurora's words hung in the air as her presence retreated into the night.

Maddie stood in front of Aiden's truck as the frigid night air rolled off the sea, whipping her hair in her face. With her husband's keys digging into her palm, she lingered at the top of the hill, staring at the Keeper's house. Light flickered inside behind the curtains, and she envisioned Jack sitting in his chair alone to ponder what had happened tonight. He'd been so nonchalant, as though this happened all the time. The beauty of Neptune Point and Haven, where she and Aiden had made memories together, now filled her with fear and unease. A single week had reshaped how she looked at the world forever, and she wanted to drive away from this place, never to return.

Jack emerged from his house, shutting the door behind him. He leaned on the porch railing, smoking his pipe as he looked in her direction. They observed each other for a moment, and with a nod, he returned inside his home.

Guided by the beam of the headlights on the winding road, she gripped the steering wheel and sobbed as she headed home. Her fingers drifted to her mouth, still tingling from Aiden's kiss, and she dried her eyes. Gabe would be upset if she arrived to pick him up with swollen eyes and a blotchy face. Resting her hand on the center console, the soft leather of Aiden's gloves touched her skin, and she held them close to her face before slipping her hands inside the fleece-lined warmth.

MADDIE, FEBRUARY 1987

DEATH OF A LIGHTHOUSE KEEPER

One year and three months had gone by since Aiden's death. Holidays and birthdays had come and gone without him waking her up to an Irish breakfast and a charming smile. It had been fifteen long months of putting one foot in front of the other, making life decisions without her partner by her side, raising their child with no one to assure her she wasn't messing him up, and an eternity of never feeling her love's arms around her again. As time passed, the physical pain of loss subsided, but the emptiness lingered like a dark cloud.

In the deep freeze of mid-February, when nothing bloomed and gray obscured the vibrance of spring, Maddie struggled to keep her magic a secret. Energy pulsed within her, begging to break free and breathe life into her world that was buried in snow and cold. She held the amulet close, tucked underneath her shirt, savoring how the jewel's power blended in harmony with her own. It possessed the same tranquil calm that had radiated from Aurora—although Maddie hadn't heard so much as a whisper since that night at Haven. Staying true to her vow to stay away from Neptune Point, the only time she saw Jack was when he came to visit her at the market, or at the launch of the Tough Cookie. She and Nellie had finally done it; they'd opened a bakery of their own.

She arranged a tray of double chocolate chip cookies that Nellie had named *Maddie's Gems* in the glass display case built into the counter, and watered the plants, resisting the urge to give in and use magic to make them bloom early.

"I can't wait until summer when we get to set up our little patio out front." Nellie wiped the display case clean of fingerprints. She leaned in close to the glass, her brows furrowed as she resprayed and wiped the glass again.

"It's clean, Nel, let's open up."

"My favorite part!" Nellie beamed as she unlocked the door and flipped the sign to 'open'.

The door swung open, sending chimes ringing against the wind. "This place is getting noticed, ladies." Theodora Tate strolled into the bakery, draped in a fur coat, and Nellie scrunched her face in disgust.

"Really, Theodora? An animal died in the name of fashion," Nellie said.

Maddie pressed her fingers against her lips to keep from chiming in. She agreed with Nellie, but Theodora Tate and her real estate firm had been pivotal in securing the property at a great price, and she didn't want to burn bridges before she'd built them.

"Good heavens, you're making my skin crawl with that pretentious name. It's just Tori, and the coat isn't real, so you can relax." She tugged her matching gloves off and wandered around the front of the bakery. "I love the mix of turquoise and gray trim in here."

"Candle smoke," Maddie said as she handed Nellie the empty tray and sidled up to Tori. Smiling at Maddie, Nellie rolled her eyes as she sashayed through the swinging kitchen door.

"Candle what?" Tori's thin eyebrow arched, and she pursed her scarlet lips, heavily lined with a pencil a shade darker.

"The shade of gray on the paint sample is called candle smoke, and that's why I chose it."

"I see. Well, I for one find it to be a good design choice regardless of the shade name." Her heeled boots clicked on the checkered tile floor as she ran a finger along the bread shelf and rubbed them together. "It's spotless, did you hire that cleaning company I told you about?"

"We are the cleaning company." Maddie rearranged the bags of sourdough bread, still warm from the early morning oven. "Once we can afford to hire one, we'll check them out."

Tori pulled a chair from the round table near the picture window. "Can I have a cup of coffee? Please. I've been told I'm not polite so I'm working on using my words. Black with one sugar packet, and one of those hazelnut pastries. I like to support local business as much as possible..." She paused, smoothing her short hair across her forehead as she eyed Maddie. "I wondered if you heard the latest news out of Neptune Point."

A sinking feeling struck Maddie's stomach as she poured coffee into a mug and stirred the sugar before placing it in front of Tori. "I haven't heard a thing, what happened?" Heat from the amulet graced her skin and her hand flew to her neck, adjusting her turtleneck sweater, concealing the jewel.

"The man that lived in the house out there, the lighthouse keeper—"

"Jack. Jack Morana." Maddie cleared her throat as her voice cracked.

"Did you know him well?" Tori raised the mug to her lips and sipped her coffee, leaving a lipstick stain on the rim of the cup. "I suppose not well enough if you weren't informed of his death."

"His what?" Maddie set a plate with the pastry on the table and slid onto the seat across from her, gripping the table to steady her racing heart. *Death?*

There had to be a mistake. Jack couldn't be dead—she'd *know*, wouldn't she?

"Don't you watch the six o'clock news?" Tori's long red nails tapped the mug as she regarded Maddie with curiosity.

"Not since Aiden..." A cold dread constricted Maddie's chest, stealing the air from her lungs. She struggled to find words among her chaotic thoughts as they tumbled back to Aiden in the living room, back to when her family was still intact and none of this mattered. "What happened to Jack?"

"So you did know him."

"He... helped me through a difficult time," Maddie whispered.

Setting the mug on the table, Tori folded her hands on the table as she leaned forward. "I'm sorry, Maddie, had I known

I would have been more tactful, please accept my apologies." Though her exterior remained cold and distant, a genuine look of compassion softened Theodora Tate's usually frigid features.

"I'm more concerned with you telling me exactly what you know."

"Well, let's see. His family couldn't get a hold of him, police went to check on him, and they found tools scattered around in the lighthouse tower. Apparently, there are storm doors surrounding the landing up there. Anyway, all signs point to him falling to his death the night of that blizzard last week. Tragic, so very, very tragic." Tori shook her head, averting her gaze from Maddie's as she reached for her mug again. "I'm waiting to see what his son will do with the property, he might need a realtor." She took another drink from her mug of coffee and dabbed her mouth with a napkin.

Maddie balled her hands in her lap, letting her nails dig into her palms to ease the magic brimming underneath her skin. "A man just died, and that's where your head goes? I'm grateful for your help with this place but be careful not to dismiss the dead so fast."

Jack Morana was gone. And she never had the chance to say goodbye.

With a graceful nod, Tori narrowed her gaze on Maddie. "While I can appreciate what you must be going through, you are a businesswoman now, too. It is my belief that we can be both compassionate and savvy, that's all I meant by my statement. I do apologize if I was out of line."

"Do you know if a funeral is planned?"

"Now that, I do not know. But I can find out." With a graceful lift of her arm, Tori eyed the gold watch around her wrist. "I better go and pick up Anna from school for an appointment." She stood and pushed her chair in. "These teen years already have me running on empty and they've just started. Enjoy this last year before Gabe turns thirteen."

"Gabe will be just fine." A ghost of a fake smile touched Maddie's lips, but her gaze drifted beyond the window. The clouds parted, revealing sunshine she hadn't seen in days. Icicles clinging to the buildings across the street sparkled as the light touched them, contrasting the darkness that had settled over her heart for the past year. And now Jack was gone too. How could she not have known of his death? There had been no signs, no warning.

"Maddie?" Tori stood with her hand on the door and tilted her head with a sigh. "You poor woman, dealing with so much loss. Listen, take care of yourself, and you know where to find me if you need anything, anything at all, I mean that. We have to stick together."

"Sure." Maddie stood, gathering the mug and plate off the table, placing them on the counter. Tori might be an impressive businesswoman, but she could use a lesson in empathy.

Swinging her coat, Tori let the door shut behind her as she strutted toward an impressive black sedan, gleaming with a mirror polish. Maddie's Buick would pale in comparison with its coating of enough dirt and salt to obscure any hint of red underneath.

There's a paint shade... Grim Death Ash.

"What are you looking at out there?" Nellie said as she sidled up to her and stared outside the glass door.

"I'm just people watching."

A man flung his scarf over his shoulder and opened the passenger door, taking Tori's hand as she stepped inside the car. He hurried into the driver's side and the car sped away, leaving a spray of slush in its wake. A pedestrian spun around and held up a middle finger, shaking his head and wiping at his coat with gloved hands.

Nellie adjusted her red-rimmed glasses and glanced at Maddie. "You doing all right? I heard about that lighthouse guy, not that I was eavesdropping—"

"Of course you were." Maddie's tone came out sharper than she intended. "I don't blame you, I'd listen too." With Nellie trailing behind, she carried the dirty dishes off the counter into the back kitchen.

"I didn't realize how close you were, I mean I know he came to the market and always bought two cupcakes, every time." The oven timer rang, and Nellie donned a pair of oven mitts.

"We weren't close, not really."

His secrets will die with him. I'm the only one alive who knows the truth about Neptune Point, and I'm not even sure how much I know.

Nellie's glasses fogged as she grabbed a tray of biscuits from the oven and placed them on a cooling rack. "You're upset, why don't you go home? Wednesdays are quiet until the lunch rush, and I can handle that on my own."

"I'm not upset—"

Nellie's voice softened. "Mads, I know you're hurting."

"You ever go through so much heartache you don't remember what contentment feels like?" Nothing made sense anymore except one thing, a fierce determination to secure a future for what little family she had left. "I'm not going home. We're going to work our assess off and turn this business into a place where locals will never forget our names, making the Tough Cookie part of their everyday conversations." Maddie retrieved an unfrosted layer cake from the large refrigerator and placed it on the counter.

"I'm right there with you, my friend."

A folded note was taped to the cover of the glass dish, and she pried it off and deciphered Nellie's handwriting.

Cake with red and pink hearts
Message: Happy 14th birthday Blythe and Enid
Delivery requested Feb. 21 to the Lighthouse Keeper's residence
at Neptune Point

Buzzing rang in Maddie's ears and heat rushed through her palms as magic reminded her of her connection to the place she'd vowed never to go back. "Did you take this cake request?"

Chimes from the front of the bakery signaled a customer, and Nellie wiped her hands on a towel as she headed toward the swinging door. "The Neptune Point cake? Sure did, yesterday. I thought you saw it in the book."

"Since when do we deliver outside of town limits?" Maddie could hardly find the air to speak. A birthday cake for two fourteen-year-olds at Jack's house?

With her hip holding the door open, Nellie nodded to someone and glanced back at Maddie. "The woman sounded flustered, I thought your lighthouse friend had family in town or something, I didn't know that he'd died." She lowered her voice. "Mads, I'm sorry, I thought you knew, I was just going to run it out Saturday morning—"

"I'll deliver it."

A soft voice called from the front of the shop, "Excuse me?"

"I gotta get this," Nellie said as she let the door swing shut behind her.

Fifteen months of avoiding Neptune Point was coming to an end.

MADDIE, FEBRUARY 1987

DEATH OF A LIGHTHOUSE KEEPER

The amulet around Maddie's neck pulsed in sync with the lighthouse beacon. Clouds threatened a morning snowfall, but beads of sweat pricked her skin as an accomplice to the persistent tingling of magic as she approached Jack's house. Balancing the square cake box, she unzipped her coat, fighting the impulse to rip the amulet from her neck and toss it into the ocean. The relentless tide of grief had mixed with the longing to rid herself of the jewel too many times since Aiden's death. Magic hadn't done a damn thing to help her. The stone's power couldn't save him back then, and she failed to see its purpose now.

The frigid winter air rushed over her exposed skin as she stretched the neck of her sweater, inhaling the sharp, salty tang of the ocean. This was her chance to meet Jack's family, ask questions about his death, and somehow find closure with a place she'd rather leave in her past forever.

With the drapes no longer covering the window, movement inside the living room caught her attention. Leaving a trail of snow prints on the porch steps, she neared the door, shifting the cake box in her arm as she raised a gloved hand to knock.

As her fist connected with the weathered wood in a swift knock, the door burst open, revealing a girl with intense amber eyes staring up at her from the shadowed interior. She appeared to be a little older than Gabe, and almost as tall. She had to be one of the birthday girls whose name was frosted on the cake; a flash of innocence filled her eyes as her gaze dropped to the pink box in Maddie's hands. "Mom, the cake is here!"

A woman with similar features as the girl appeared with a smile. "Invite her inside, Enid, it's freezing. Put the cake on the table, please, but don't open the box yet." She ruffled the girl's dark, chin-length hair, revealing a tiny scar along her cheek. "I'm Rosalie Morana, thank you for delivering the cake. The girl on the phone told me you didn't usually offer delivery service so we appreciate the exception."

"No problem." Maddie stepped inside as the girl took the cake from her hands. She pulled her gloves off and tucked them in her coat pocket. Heat coursed from the amulet along her skin, and she pressed her hand against her sweater to keep it hidden. Jack's chair was gone—*all* of Jack's furniture was gone. New plush furniture was arranged around the fireplace with a polished coffee table in the center of a brightly patterned area rug. The living room was transformed into a space that looked like it was torn from a magazine, leaving Maddie speechless and on the verge of tears. It was as though Jack had been erased.

Another girl approached with a grimace, revealing a scar that mirrored Enid's jagged line etched into her cheek. "Who are you?"

"Maddie Harlow—"

"Blythe, manners, please." Rosalie Morana raised her eyebrows at her daughter before glancing back at Maddie. "I'm sorry about the chaos in here today." She tucked her sleek hair behind her ears and crossed her arms. "We're trying to have some sort of birthday party for the girls, but my father-in-law just passed."

The girl named Blythe rolled her eyes as a little boy came bounding down the winding staircase and rushed to the piano at the bottom. With a mischievous grin, he played the keys like a seasoned pianist, each note echoing in the room, creating a haunting melody. Maddie almost hummed along, catching herself. Aurora's ghostly voice had once carried this song.

"Ezra, stop!" Blythe said. "Mom, you said he'd stay upstairs when everyone comes to the party."

"Ben's going to take him upstairs when Dad brings him home, Ez won't bother you at all." Rosalie glared at the little boy who covered his mouth as he laughed uncontrollably, chasing Blythe into the kitchen.

"Your son's very talented," Maddie said. "I've heard that song before—"

"It's from a music book he found, Lila..." Rosalie's eyes darted from the piano back to Maddie. "My mother-in-law used to play."

The mention of Jack's name again, combined with the transformation to his once silent house, now alive as his family bustled around the main floor, gripped Maddie with an ache of grief. How much grief and heartbreak could someone stand before they drowned in it? The warmth and vibrance of joy had long since bled out, leaving behind an emptiness of what those emotions felt like in her memory. "I'm sorry for your loss, Jack was a nice man."

"Well, it's been months since we last saw him, we had no idea his mobility declined so much. But the man refused to leave this place even when we told him it was too much for him. You knew him?"

Better than you think.

"I did... He was my friend."

Rosalie gestured toward the piano as her dark eyes lifted to the top of the stairs. "I'm going to try and make it feel like home, but it'll take time. My husband is his only child, and his mom died five years ago. I didn't want this big house, and I want to seal up that door in the basement—who builds a tunnel underground, anyway? Gives me the creeps if I'm honest, but he refuses to sell it, so here we are."

She sure had redesigned the living room in a hurry. Maddie exhaled and stood near the closed front door. A spirit had killed Aiden. Perhaps he'd done the same to Jack. If the darkness had returned, she needed to know. "I hope I'm not being inappropriate, but what happened to him?"

"Oh, um." With her arms still folded across her chest, Rosalie leaned toward Maddie. "He fell off the tower, I can't even talk about it without crying." She dabbed her eyes, careful not to smudge her mascara. "I don't know much about taking care of a lighthouse, but his toolbox was up there, and the police think he was replacing a bulb, or cleaning the lens? We're not sure, but whatever he was doing, he ended up outside because the door was open, and he was just... gone." A sob caught in her throat.

"He fell?" Maddie whispered, careful not to let her voice carry to Jack's grandchildren, and Rosalie only nodded with tears in her eyes. Jack knew this place too well to fall off the lighthouse, unless he'd made the decision himself... Or something even more sinister had happened to him.

A headache thumped from the front of her head down the back and she rubbed her neck. "What about a funeral?"

"It was just family, he was cremated, his wishes." Rosalie's fingers trailed along her chin and down her neck. "The twins' birthday party is in a couple hours—"

Maddie held a hand up. She'd come to drop off a cake and leave, and Neptune Point made her uneasy. "I'll go. Thanks for being so open when you don't know me from a bar of soap."

A smile crinkled the corners of Rosalie's eyes as she smiled. "A friend of Jack Morana is always welcome here."

Maddie didn't want to return to Jack's house. She wanted to stay far away from Neptune Point. This place had taken more from her than anything else ever could. "I should get back to the bakery, enjoy the cake today."

As Maddie turned, a soft voice spoke behind her. "Don't forget this." Enid held up a milk crate by the handles.

"What is it?" Maddie said.

Rosalie shrugged. "Just some of Jack's stuff we gathered for donation, if you'd like to have it, it's all yours." She knitted her brows together and glanced at her daughter. "Maddie might not want it, honey."

With an intensity that bordered on mystical like her grandfather, Enid's amber eyes never left Maddie's face as she set the plastic box on the floor. "He said you'd come and he wants you to have it," she whispered.

"I think she doesn't want me giving her granddad's things away to strangers," Rosalie said. "Maddie, thank you for dropping off the cake. You have my word I'll be a regular at the Tough Cookie, especially now that we're going to be locals." She made a face as she spoke, and dishes clattered from the kitchen. "I better see what those two are up to before they kill each other."

"Don't worry about me, I'm leaving in just a second." Maddie bent down and traced the colorful pattern of gold-edged flowers on the floral teapot, nestled amongst a stack of books filling the box. "He said I'd come, did he. You can hear him?"

"Sometimes, but don't tell anyone. My brother gets mad at me when I say anything about it, but he's an asshole."

"The little boy that was here, Ezra? He seems so sweet—"

"Not him, my older brother." Enid sighed. "He just doesn't get it, that's all. He hated Granddad, called him bad names."

Maddie glanced toward the voices coming from the kitchen, and back to Enid. A cold knot tightened in her chest. "What sort of names?"

"I don't know, it doesn't matter anymore, right?" Enid picked up the crate and handed it to Maddie. "Here, take it home."

As Maddie clutched the crate's handles, Enid opened the front door and a gust of icy air swept Maddie's hair into her eyes. "Tell him I said thank you," Maddie said as she stepped onto the porch.

"Don't need to, he hears you." With a broad smile, Enid waved, shutting the door.

Maddie hurried to the car as snow blew sideways, lashing against it with every gust of ocean air. The milk crate filled with Jack's belongings clattered on the passenger seat as she slammed the door and rushed around to the driver's side. Breathless, she slid into the seat and stuck the keys in the ignition, bringing the engine to life as she cranked the heat and angled the vents to melt frost off the windshield.

If you can hear me, where are you, Jack?

Yanking the box closer, she picked up the teapot and something rattled inside. A sharp pain shot through her finger as she removed the lid, cutting herself on a jagged edge. Flinching, she stuck her bleeding finger in her mouth and pulled her glove out of her pocket to apply pressure. The ceramic carafe contained a broken piece from the teapot lid and a gold pocket watch. Turning the broken piece of the teapot between her thumb and forefinger, she silently promised Jack she'd fix it as soon as she got home. She pressed the broken piece of glass against the rough edge of the teapot lid. With a little glue, it would be a perfect fit.

Retrieving the pocket watch, she let the weight settle in her palm. Curved lines were etched deep in the gold on the back of the watch cover with a tall rectangular shape in the center. She held the watch up to the window, comparing the similarities to the lighthouse as its beacon rotated against the gray sky. Her finger traced tiny, engraved trees at the edge of the gold cover, her eyes drifting toward the pathway leading to Haven.

This is a map of Neptune Point.

The watch resisted as she pried it open, and her heart sank as she read the inscription on the inside of the case. *Morana.*

"Goodbye, Jack," she whispered as she tucked the watch in her pocket and wiped her eyes.

She should have driven away, back home to the bakery where she'd left Gabe with Nellie, but one of the larger books in the box caught her eye. "Neptune Point History" was emblazoned in crimson ink across the worn, hard cover. The pages crinkled as she flipped them, briefly pausing at black and white photos showcasing the lighthouse being built in the late 1800s, including images of men standing outside the lighthouse beaming with pride, and gathering around the kerosene lamp in the center of the landing with a caption that said, 'Neptune Point Lighthouse of Aurora, lantern room'. She skimmed past detailed descriptions of the 'cupola', a domed style roof design they'd used, but none of the words on the page held her attention.

As she started to close the book, the pages fluttered, stopping on a grainy photograph of a woman standing behind a group of men on the lighthouse landing. Maddie froze, and held the book open wider, tilting it near the window for a better view. A hint of a smile graced the woman's face as a flash of violet light reflected off the nearby glass, illuminating her mystical eyes. She looked as though she was on the verge of laughter as the men devoted their attention to papers in their hands. Maddie lifted the page closer to her eyes, examining the woman's long dark hair held back on one side with a raven-shaped metal hairpin. But it was the soft, warm glow emanating from the object clutched in the woman's fingers against her wide collar that held Maddie's captivated gaze.

As she let the book drop in her lap, still open to the page with the photograph, Maddie's fingers reached to her own neck, curling around the amulet. The woman staring back at her, wearing the same amulet around her neck over a century ago, was Aurora. Magic pulsed against her skin, spreading through her chest like a rush of warm water.

With the low hum of the engine vibrating through the car, she tucked the book back into the milk crate and untied the frayed rope binding a smaller book as the pages threatened to spill out. She traced her fingers over journal entries written in cursive handwriting, reading various dates growing closer together as she turned the pages, all belonging to the year 1895.

The pages overflowed with poems, love letters, and spells of magic and fire. The last page triggered a crawling sensation that spread over her body like spiders had escaped a disturbed web and taken up residence underneath her coat.

A fire shall come with his death. And mine.

Love, Aurora

A large truck rounded the corner, sending a spray of powdery snow into the air. Maddie secured the rope around the book and placed it back in the box beside her. A young man, perhaps a few years older than Gabe, glared at her as the truck roared past along the snow-packed driveway. Frost on the window obscured his features, but he held his vacant stare on her as they drove away.

I need to get the hell away from this place.

Her knuckles paled as she gripped the steering wheel and accelerated onto the coastal road, but a shadow flew over the windshield with a deep gurgling croak, causing her to swerve. The wipers squealed back and forth as she veered off the road, breathless with her heart hammering in her chest. As she leaned forward, scanning the road, a large black bird—bigger than any crow she'd ever seen—landed on her car hood, ruffling its feathers.

"Jesus mercy... *shit*." The wipers' steady rhythm cleared snow off the window, allowing her a clear line of sight to the graceful bird perched on her car.

With a stem clutched in its beak, the bird carried a flower closer to the windshield. It was a lotus flower like the ones that had appeared in the Coda River the night she'd helped banish Aiden's killer into an unknown abyss.

The bird extended its wings and lifted off the hood of the car, releasing the flower as it flew away. Maddie stepped out and picked up the wilting flower. Golden light spun from the amulet hanging over her jacket, and the magic coursing through her hands felt like a thousand tiny sparks. The wilting flower trembled in her palm, unfurling its petals and dissolving into the wings of a bright blue butterfly that vanished as it fluttered skyward.

Heavy silence pressed in on her, only broken by the muffled constant sweep of the windshield wipers. The amulet thrummed with magic before fading into a dark stillness. She was bound by the light of the Sisterhood, but darkness would never be far behind. Protecting the only family she had left was all that mattered.

She was a witch. A mystic who had the power to heal and breathe life, but using her abilities would only attract danger and pain. As she stood on the side of the road near the bridge leading away from Neptune Point, she vowed to leave this place behind and never use magic again.

FOURTEEN

AURORA, 1895

THE END OF AN ERA

S leep eluded Aurora the night of a full moon, and this late August evening was no exception. With hauntings growing more persistent and promises of death plaguing her, she had no choice but to prepare for his arrival once again. How many times could she send him back through the gate only to have it open again?

Silk and linen fabric rustled against her hands as she gathered the skirts of her favorite black dress that her husband often deemed, "fit for a funeral," and gently closed the door to her bedroom, leaving his sleeping form behind. He was the love of her life—the man who walked alongside her in this life and forever, who knew of her magic and loved her enough to carry her into an eternity.

She paused to check in on each of her children as they slept, kissing her fingers and touching their foreheads before tiptoeing out of each bedroom. They would forever be her greatest legacy, and her love for her family was so profound that she would surrender her own life to ensure theirs. She'd been blessed with more precious years than she dreamed possible, given the constant threat of simply being a gifted mystic, but as she rounded the staircase and her feet graced the living room at the bottom, dread filled her heart.

Her fingers brushed the wooden piano, and she closed her eyes, longing to play the music resonating in her soul. A quiet hum escaped her lips as she smiled, recalling holidays gone by and celebrations of her children's first milestones.

She sat on a plush chair, pulling it against the dining room table, and untied the smooth rope securing her journal. Darkness lurked, waiting for her, hunting her, and she had a message to leave behind should he win this time. She dipped the nib of her pen into the bottle of ink and tapped it on the glass as she opened the book to a new page.

Angling the pen, she wrote in a frantic rhythm. The metal scraped over the rough paper until her fingers cramped and her wrist ached. With a sharp metallic clang, the chimes of the grandfather clock in the corner rang out their warning. As her fingers wandered along the butterflies and vines engraved in the wood, the amulet around her neck emitted a vibrant purple light, its heat a searing wave that spread down her arms. And despite the Sisterhood's magic and the fire's warmth radiating from the hearth, icy air enveloped her, and with each shallow breath, a small cloud of mist appeared before her. His presence, heavy with menace, had returned, and this time, she was determined to stop him.

The chimes silenced, replaced by a hushed chorus of a thousand whispers. Their words crystallized, each syllable distinct and resonant, as if the air itself had sharpened. Spell magic had protected her home and family for over a decade, but he had found a way beyond the wards. The Sisterhood had at last perfected a spell to condemn the witch hunter into an everlasting netherworld, locking the gate forever. The heavy weight of responsibility settled on her as an urgent need to protect her daughters and generations of witches to come ignited a fierce surge of power flowing through her.

It has always been my prophecy to bear, for as long as there are those who seek to harm us.

Gripping the pen with trembling fingers, she dipped it back into the inkwell to end her last passage in the book.

A fire shall come with his death. And mine.

Love, Aurora

Her laced boots tapped on the wooden floor at a quiet pace as she rose from the table and headed outside, shutting the door behind her with a soft click. Placing her hand against the door, she recited a last protection spell and stepped off the veranda, inhaling the sea air as it rolled off the ocean.

The moon's silver light illuminated the ocean spray as it dispersed into the air like shards of glass from a shattered chandelier. A frigid gray mist spun along the jagged rocks, and the mournful cries of seagulls carried over the thunderous surf in the darkness as they woke from their slumber.

He had come for her.

An intense surge of power flashed from the amulet, rushing through her fingers into her chest as Aurora clasped the vibrant jewel. With a sharp inhale, she welcomed the familiar sensation of magic coursing through her. A funnel of water churned and rose from the sea before slamming over the rocks, trickling onto the ground near her feet.

Aurora approached the lighthouse entrance and held the amulet away from her neck, directing a stream of swirling gold light toward the witch hunter as he materialized into a version of the man he had once been.

Hunter of witches.

The hood of his cloak fell to his shoulders, revealing a grotesquely contorted head tilted at an unnatural angle, the vacant eyes glaring at her as though they could pierce her soul. Her throat tightened, cutting off her ability to breathe, but she fought back, channeling magic from the women who had met their deaths before her. The amulet released a stream of light, swirling around her and returning air into her lungs.

His cloak billowed around his boots as he rushed toward her, releasing a horrifying, grating moan, but this time she refused to run from him.

This time, she would be responsible for his demise.

Opening the heavy door to the lighthouse, she ascended the winding staircase to the landing. This was *her* beacon of light, her *home*.

His presence was an oppressive shadow, haunting and threatening her. And like a beast stalking his prey, he would pursue her to the death.

A defiant smile played on her lips as she rushed through the door to stand outside and grasped the railing. Gusts of wind ripped at her dress and sent her hair flying around her head in a halo of black strands as an ominous figure loomed behind her.

"A fiery grave awaits you and others of your kind, *witch*," he hissed and extended a clawed hand toward her throat. "I shall reclaim the jewel adorned on your neck."

"You will do no such thing, hate has no place here." She sidestepped his desperate grab with fingers twisted like the roots of a dead tree, scraping against the air as he lunged for the amulet.

The amulet's essence pulsed around her in a vibrant indigo light as warm air caressed her face, extending down her body. Voices whispered the enchantment, their words weaving a shield to protect her from the suffocating darkness. Stepping onto the landing in a kaleidoscope of colors, the spirits of the Sisterhood appeared, drowning Aurora's fear.

"Death's hand seeks you, Heath Hathorne," she said, her voice unwavering as the raw power coursed through her like the Coda River.

A burning sensation twisted in Aurora's lungs as she breathed deeply, channeling the Sisterhood's energy. Harnessing the familiar magic, she pulled the string of her power like a taut bow, unleashing a deadly weapon as fiery power coursed through her.

The air crackled like a lightning storm as a shimmering vortex of light appeared. A ribbon of purple stretched from the amulet, constricting around the witch hunter. His eyes narrowed into slits and his face contorted into a grotesque mask of fury mixed with fear as the light dragged his body toward the moon gate. Flames engulfed his hands as his boots hit the wooden floor. His lips curled into a tight, unnatural grin that held a silent threat of cruelty and a dark satisfaction of malicious intent. Ripping the silver chain from her neck, Aurora stepped closer. Her chest heaved, each magic-filled breath sending waves of heat from the gem she held inches from his face. With a calculating glint in his vacant gaze, he seized the necklace from her fingers as he plunged over the edge of the lighthouse.

"No!" Aurora screamed. Her dress snagged on the railing as she whirled around, and she grabbed handfuls of fabric, tearing herself free as she fled down the staircase below.

Stumbling over uneven gravel and moss, she raced toward the unforgiving, rocky shoreline. The beacon swept light across the sky, casting shadows that followed her every frantic step, and illuminating Hathorne's cloak as he paced along the treacherous rocks. As long as the amulet remained within his death grasp, he would possess unimaginable power. The jewel could never belong to such wickedness, and she would rather die than let him hurt another soul.

He tilted his head from side to side and stared at her with unblinking eyes as the amulet dangled from his long, clawed finger. As the black jewel swayed in the wind, the last of its inner light flickered and died, leaving it dark and lifeless.

Searing magic tingled along Aurora's face and down her arms, burning into her palms. "You have stolen from me—from us. We shall reclaim what is rightfully ours." The cliffs behind him appeared to rise like guardians as the waves crashed against them. A current of electricity coursed along her skin as she approached him with her hands poised for attack.

The Sisterhood's spell flowed from her lips; each word infused with power. "Essence of night. Where the water flows. The peak of the moon's power. Calling upon those who have burned—"

He opened his mouth, a low groan building into a deafening roar that vibrated in her chest as he charged. His hand tightened around her throat, choking the air from her lungs. "There shall be no salvation for your kind here."

I shall not die until his wrath has ended.

The amulet hanging within his deathly grip brushed against Aurora's cheek, and her skin prickled as the air grew thick with mystic energy. With strangled gasps and a surge of power gathered in her hands, she wrapped her fingers around the jewel, igniting a burst of purple light. The witch hunter's grip faltered as an iridescent, swirling mass of shadows bent and flickered behind him.

Ghostly silhouettes of the Sisterhood moved past her, dragging him into the infinite void as their unified melodic voices recited the rest of the spell. *"Vanquish harm by the grace of the water's reflection—"*

"Lock the door, seeking haven for all," she said as their words faded beyond the moon gate's entrance. A spiraling thread of light glowed deep within the amulet's core as it rested in her palm.

The edges of the gate blurred as the passage to another world shimmered and dissolved. A deathly hush fell over Hathorne as he lingered for one last moment and an unnerving stillness shrouded him on the other side.

"Please leave me in peace," she muttered. As she lifted the silver chain to place the jewel around her neck, Hathorne released a fiery explosion that shook the ground, and the necklace escaped her hold, falling to the ground. The gate collapsed, trapping him inside, but a scream tore from her chest as the fire consumed her dress, burning her skin and hair with agonizing heat.

She slipped away from her body, and her eyes welled with tears as memories of her life as a lighthouse keeper flooded her mind. Standing on the landing watching the sunset with her husband's arms around her, sharing candlelit dinners and endless conversations drifting into the morning hours, teaching her daughters how to create music on the grand piano, and years of laughter echoing through the walls of her home offered a bittersweet comfort.

A fire shall come with his death. And mine.

Her own prophecy proved true.

Death marked the end of Aurora's journey as part of the living, yet life had moved forward for those she had left behind. With each step along the banks of Neptune Point, the sun sparkled over the water. The rhythmic thud of an axe echoed through the backyard of the large Keeper's house as a man chopped wood, sending splinters flying.

Aurora's granddaughter, now a striking woman bearing her mother's kind eyes and genuine heart, carried a mug outside to the gentleman, and his face beamed as he brought the cup to his lips. Laughter filled the air as their child ran through the tall grass, holding onto kite strings. The image of a black bird decorated the purple fabric at the end of its long rope tether, dipping across the sky with each gust of wind.

Her family's legacy would eternally bind Aurora's soul to this place, and she would forever keep watch. Her fingers reached for the amulet around her neck as she approached the house she had once called home. The lasting power of the spell she had used to quell her offspring's magic remained a mystery, yet a quiet sense of relief had settled over Aurora, knowing her family would be free from harm.

A strange ache encircled her lifeless heart with a *knowing*. Those blessed with magic should have the freedom to choose how to embrace their gifts, and yet, Aurora had taken control of her daughters' calling to breathe life, saving the ones who needed help on the other side. The consequences of her actions would mean an endless search for a purpose that no longer existed for them, where they would find emptiness instead of soul fulfillment.

I had to keep them safe, it was the only way.

Whispers of the Sisterhood called to her. *"Others will come, needing our help. It does not end here with them, not in this town."*

With one last lingering gaze at her granddaughter's family, Aurora's ghostly form faded from Neptune Point, and her feet sank into the soft, warm sand of a place she knew only as peace.

Part Two
2010

Maddie Harlow
&
Enid Morana

FIFTEEN

ENID 2010

Waking up dead had been like gasping for air after being held under water. If Ben hadn't shoved her out of the boat, making sure she never resurfaced, maybe she'd breathe real air into her alive self again. She could still see the cruel smirk plastered across his face as she sank underneath the dark, cold water. There had to be someone out there who could help her uncover the truth. She wouldn't rest until she found another soul who'd be able to see her.

But blood no longer pulsed along Enid's neck and wrists, and time stretched through a layer of fog, the years moving too fast, but too slowly, with flickers of memories from the life she'd once had, glimpses of who she used to be, and the dreams she had but never got the chance to fulfill. Never had her first kiss, never fell in love, never attended college to become... *anything*. She kept waiting to feel normal again, to feel her heart beating and her lungs expanding in her chest. Even pain would be a welcome change from nothingness—anything to feel alive again.

I'll be sixteen forever.

Trees swayed and seagrass rippled like water under the moonlight as a breeze rolled off the ocean toward the forest. Longing to feel the summer night air against her skin, Enid pushed up the sleeves of her heart-covered sweater, a present from her twin sister for their last birthday.

Well, for my last birthday.

Blythe would be an adult now, perhaps living with a new family somewhere else, since no one had returned to the Keeper's house. But she would never see her sister again; not until she died, and Enid hoped with her entire being that her sister got to live the life that Ben had stolen from herself and Ezra. The ache of loneliness washed over her as she gripped the rail of the lighthouse landing, unable to feel the wind or the cool metal underneath her hands, caught between two worlds. Sadness and anger blended, haunting her like the constant ringing her mother's crystal glasses made when she traced the edges with a finger, annoying the hell out of her.

Ben had murdered his own siblings, and she refused to let go, remaining in between the living and dead until the world knew what their brother had done. He'd stolen her life, her little brother's life. Everyone had been oblivious, calling it an accident. He had directed his intense hatred at her from the day they moved into the Keeper's house and she'd discovered her magic was more powerful than she realized. The way Ben had lurked around the lighthouse, watching her for months, should've been a warning sign, but their parents brushed off his threats as sibling rivalry... If rivalry and vengeance collided.

Passing through the glass doors inside, she entered the silent light room, where an automated lamp cast a rotating beam of light. Thick dust coated the metal shutters of the small windows, and as she brushed away cobwebs, her hand passed through the stone. Cleaning the tower ledges had been her least favorite chore, but now she'd give anything to feel the grime on her fingers. She tugged her sleeves back down over her once radiant, sun-kissed skin, now pale like the dead girl she was, somehow disturbing a spider as it dashed across its tattered web.

She leaned closer to the web as the spider stopped and curled its legs together. "How can you feel my presence, and I can touch my sweater, but nothing else?"

With arms outstretched like an airplane, Ezra appeared, sprinting up the winding staircase and around the landing. His chestnut hair flopped in his eyes as he charged along the railing. "Think I could fly right off this lighthouse and dive into the ocean?"

"Probably, but why would you want to do that?"

"Because I'm already dead and there's nothing to do here." He stopped running, but his chest didn't move. If he'd been alive, he'd be breathless, panting from his exertion. "Enid, why don't we get to see Mom anymore? She died, we saw the purple lady take her. Daddy and Blythe left, but where did Ben go?"

Enid balled her fists at her sides, digging her nails into flesh she couldn't feel, remembering the sharp sensation in the absence of physical pain. "Ben should be in jail or dead for what he did to us."

A deep frown creased Ezra's face as his amber eyes widened. "You've got hate in your heart, you gotta make that go away, it won't help, not here, not anymore." He wrapped his arms around her and buried his face against her sweater. The closest they could get to a hug in their ghostly states was a subtle warmth where their energies intertwined.

"I don't hate, I just want the truth to be told, and I can't leave here until I find a way to make that happen, that's all."

"You didn't answer why I can't see Mom anymore." Letting her go, Ezra circled the lighthouse lamp.

"I don't really know, but she went to a beautiful place, Ez, and I'll make sure you get back to her, I promise."

The vision of a woman in a long black gown as she disappeared with her mother into the horizon slipped further from Enid's mind, along with her memories of being alive. The years that had passed between their mother's death and their own remained a mystery. Something inside of her wanted to break free from her earthly life and cut the tether holding her to Neptune Point. Her soul needed to escape the pain she clung to, pressing her to disconnect from her previous life, but she couldn't let that happen.

I need him to pay for what he did.

Her eyes blurred with sudden tears, and she touched her face, but their sting on her cheeks only came to her through a memory of the last time she'd cried.

Ben killed a seagull and laughed as it suffered in my arms.

"I think she's happy there." Ezra crouched in front of the lamp and the powerful beam reflected gold in his eyes.

Enid had begged Ezra to go with the woman in the purple light, but he wouldn't leave her side and now it was too late.

They were both trapped in an existence between the living and the dead, and his fate was in her hands as much as her own.

"You should've gone with her when you had the chance, you shouldn't be here."

Defiance flashed across his pale face, and his brown eyes sparkled. "You shouldn't be here either."

"I need to be here, and I will find someone who can help."

"I can go wherever I want," Ezra said. "I hear her calling me and I follow her voice."

Enid placed her hands on his small shoulders and narrowed her eyes at him. "Then next time, stay, and don't come back."

He shrugged away from her. "I can't stay, not while you're still *here*." Turning toward the glass door, he reached for the handle. "You can touch things like when we were alive, you know, just think real hard about what it used to feel like, and it works. I practiced, look." His hand grasped the handle, and the door gave way as he pulled. He glanced over his shoulder with a wide smile before rushing outside. With arms outstretched, he stood on a cement ledge. A whirlwind of sea air surrounded him as he let out a joyful shout before spiraling over the edge and disappearing into a brilliant mist of shimmering light.

Enid hurried through the open door, leaning over the railing. Waves thundered with each surge against the rocks below, sending up spray that misted over a raven perched on a branch near the boarded-up Keeper's house. With a rustle of its shaggy

The door creaked open, and a sleepy-eyed Drew stumbled in, clutching a blanket. "What are you doing?"

She rubbed her eyes as Maddie tucked the amulet beneath her shirt and kicked the book under the bed. "I thought you were sleeping."

"I heard a scary yell." Drew glanced up, her eyes locking with Enid's. "She came back."

"She's leaving," Maddie said with a smile, brushing away the damp strands of hair clinging to Drew's face. "I told you I'm going to take care of it. Come on, I'll tuck you back in." With a glance over her shoulder, Maddie walked Drew out of the room, taking the amulet with her.

A magnetic pull dragged Enid away from the house and back to Neptune Point. The beacon of light spun around in the lighthouse tower as she stood on the rocks below overlooking the vast ocean. The crashing waves sprayed seawater into the night sky, mimicking the stars.

A sudden gust of wind tossed her hair, swirling around her like she was in the eye of a hurricane, but when she held her hands in the air, she felt nothing. She'd found a sliver of hope, a human connection to the living world. For a moment today, the weight of her tragic death had lifted from her shoulders, giving her a fleeting taste of freedom.

She refused to let go until the truth was set free, or she'd be stuck here forever.

MADDIE 2010

Gabe finished mowing the lawn and sat on the steps with a beer in his hand, watching Drew wobble down the driveway on her tricycle. Maddie pushed the porch swing with her foot, creaking along with the rhythmic squeak of the bike's wheels. The evenings had cooled over the past week with the end of August approaching, ending the heatwave, and Gabe's return home from sea brought a need for Maddie to know what would be next for his daughter.

With the sunset gleaming on the crystal stones Maddie had arranged by the front door, she bent down and concealed them beneath the welcome mat. The protection spell she'd used with a little help from the book and the amulet had kept the dead girl's chill away, silencing Drew's constant chatter about Enid, but guilt had pushed Maddie to spend three days digging into the Morana tragedy at Neptune Point.

The children's mother had taken her own life not long after their deaths, and their father had left town with Blythe. Ben Morana had disappeared without a trace or a body to be found, as though he'd never existed, but Maddie remembered him on the day she'd delivered the birthday cake when he had passed her in a truck with his father.

Investigators ruled out foul play in Enid and Ezra's deaths, deeming it a terrible boating accident. One newspaper article she'd found at the library was an interview from the early 90s with a young man who claimed Ben had left town permanently to escape his devastation over the loss of his siblings. If Ben Morana had been responsible for killing his brother and sister, what could Maddie do about it? She had no evidence other than a dead girl—and no police officer would believe or entertain that as a fact. Ben Morana could be dead himself at this point. Keeping Enid away from Drew was her only priority.

"I need to talk to you." Leaning against a wooden post, Gabe shifted on the step to face her.

Drew rode her bike to the edge of the lawn and hopped off to chase a butterfly. Her carefree laughter carried over the distant hush of waves lapping Jupiter Cove Beach.

"You're not staying in town, are you?" Maddie stopped swinging as she sat up straight and folded her hands in her lap.

"I can't, Mom. I need the money, and it pays well." Gabe ran a hand over his stubbled face, the red in his beard matching his untamed hair. As he dropped his hand, shifting his gaze toward Drew, his profile resembled that of his father's.

A wave of grief crept into Maddie's chest. Time did nothing to lessen grief's control, ambushing her when she least expected and staying for as long as it pleased.

"Any word from her mom?" she asked.

Gabe's face reddened, blending with the smattering of freckles across his cheeks. "If you count divorce papers in the mail from a California address giving me full custody, otherwise, nope. Nothing. Not a goddam word or a phone call. I think she's staying with her mom, but who fucking knows."

"You swore." Drew ran up to her father, clasping her hands over her mouth.

"It's okay, sweetheart, Daddy's just talking with Gran." Gabe offered a strained smile, masking the sadness in his eyes. "Why don't you bike some more and practice for when I get you a bigger one. I'll teach you to ride it."

Drew threw her arms around him, and he hesitated before embracing her in a tight hug. She pulled away and twirled as she skipped back to her tricycle.

"Don't make promises you can't keep." A hot, angry flush rose in Maddie's face. She shoved her grief aside and stared at her son. Gabe had his dad's physical features, but Aiden would never have left his family behind for anything.

"I'm not, Mom, Jesus."

"She lost her mom, don't you put her through losing her dad too."

"I'm not leaving her, I would never do what Joelle did—"

"What did you want to talk to me about?"

He let his head fall against the post, averting his eyes. "I'm supposed to leave next week for three months, but I'll be back before Christmas." His head lifted to face Maddie again. "They need a marine engineer on board. It's a good opportunity, it's what I studied for. Dad would be proud of me." He lowered his voice as Drew rode in circles, making tire tracks in the gravel. "I'm all she's got now and I'm no good if I can't take care of her. I need this job to do that."

Maddie got up from the swing and sat beside Gabe on the porch steps, stretching her legs in front of her. As crickets chirped their evening music, a breeze carried the sweet scent of lavender. Lifting her feet, Drew let her bike roll over a bump in the driveway, stomping on the pedals before coasting to the end of the driveway.

I need to become her home.

"Your right about one thing, Dad would be proud," Maddie said. "But you're also very wrong, Gabe."

"About what?"

"You're not all she's got, love. She has me too, and so do you."

Gabe's shoulders relaxed and his chest heaved. "You'll take care of her for me? You don't mind?"

"I'll take care of her, but it's not just for you, she's my family too. I love you, but don't you dare abandon her like Joelle did. Trust is a fine line, Gabe. You'll lose her if you break it, and that'll be on you."

"I won't." He exhaled a sigh of relief. "Thanks, Mom. You're saving us."

"Yeah, yeah," Maddie said, standing. She grasped the handle of the lawn mower to wheel it into the shed, but Gabe rose and stopped her.

"I'm serious," he said. "Things have been shitty as hell since Joelle left. I've been drinking too much, not focused... I'm sorry I need you so damn much."

Maddie embraced him, giving him a pat on the back. "Don't be sorry for needing someone, we all do. Take care of yourself and get your ass back in this house for Christmas with a new bike for your daughter."

As Maddie pushed the lawn mower into the shed, Drew's bike tipped over, sending her sprawling onto the ground. Gabe rushed to her side, gathering her into his arms. He comforted her with a soothing tone as Drew wiped her tear-streaked face and he set her on the porch swing. Examining her bloody knee, he kissed her forehead before darting inside.

Holding back from running to her granddaughter and taking over, Maddie busied herself with the lock on the shed door. If he was going to be away for months at a time, she'd let him be a dad whenever he was home.

Drew sniffled, watching blood trickle down her scraped knee as Gabe returned with a first aid kit. He cleaned the wound and placed a bandage over the cut, making a silly face as he talked to her. Drew chewed on her bottom lip until a chuckle burst free and a grin crossed her face. He kissed her bandaged knee, and took her hand, leading her inside the house.

Gabe just had to figure things out, and he'd be back. Maddie knew her son, and he loved his daughter, but heartbreak consumed him. Once he found a way to move on from Joelle, he'd come back and take care of his family, and everything would return to normal. Maddie had to believe her son would do the right thing, eventually.

Twenty

Enid 2010

Standing near the Coda River's edge, Enid held her hands up and recited versions of spells she could remember from her days of playing with magic. She focused her intention on returning to Drew and Maddie, but a cement wall kept her away, like a fortress blocking her out. Flashes of lightning crackled bright against dark clouds as she summoned the Sisterhood, using the words that had appeared in Maddie's spell book.

"The Sisterhood shall never leave you," Enid called out into the empty forest clearing. "Hello? Sisterhood? *Anyone?*"

Thunder rumbled through the forest, and another snap of lighting streaked the night sky, highlighting the green tree-tops. "Someone must be around to help, come on!"

"What are you doing?" Ezra used two sticks to pick up rocks and toss them into the water.

"I'm trying to get back to the girl who can see me, but I think her grandmother used a spell to keep me away. I should've taken the amulet back—"

"It's not supposed to be like this," Ezra said. "It's not right."

"You know what's not right, Ez? Where'd Ben go? Have you seen him anywhere, because I sure haven't, which means he's not dead! He shouldn't get a second chance at life when we're stuck here, it's not fair."

"We're not stuck!" Ezra threw the sticks, and they bounced off the water before the current dragged them downstream. "I see Mom all the time now, and you can too. We don't have to stay here."

"I'm not leaving until Ben is in jail or dead."

"And I'm not leaving until *you* do, so we are stuck, I guess." He crossed his arms and pouted as he trekked over a bed of dried pine needles, kicking them away. "That purple lady gave you a necklace, why don't you just use that? It's magic."

"It's gone, she has it."

"Who?"

"Maddie, Drew's grandmother... Doesn't matter." Enid sat on a boulder and let her fingers dip in the water, focusing on the numbing cold of the current as it tugged at her hand. She clung to the exhilaration of being alive again with human flesh, but without the pain. The minute she let it go, a ghostly shimmer consumed her, and a pull from the other side beckoned for her to leave this place. She wasn't supposed to be here, but she couldn't move on. Not while he was still free.

If she lost contact with Drew and Maddie forever, who else could help her in the world of the living? Fragments of memories edged her mind with a vision of her last birthday party before life came to an abrupt end. When everyone else had left that day, Enid's best friend Celeste had joined her on the lighthouse landing. They'd considered leaving Atlas Cliffs, becoming roommates in college in a big city one day. A sudden, undeniable truth from her past life crept into her death. Enid and Celeste had known they were already a part of the Sisterhood a long time ago.

There are others.

"You know, I had a friend who was like me. I bet she'd be able to see me if I could just..."

Use my magic like a telephone.

"Stop it." Ezra wrapped his arms around her, hugging her as his slight frame sparkled and faded. "Come with me?" He retreated with his hand outstretched, but she shook her head as he disappeared.

"You are a persistent one." Aurora emerged from a haze of purple mist. Wisps of smoke curled from her singed hair and dress.

"Why don't you help me then?" Enid turned her back to the woman and folded her arms across her chest.

"My dear, this is not my journey, it is yours. My capabilities are finite and there are limits to magic."

Enid's hair tickled her chin, and she gathered a strand around her finger, pulling it tight to feel the sensation on her skin before letting it go.

Aurora glided closer, cradling Enid's face in her hands. "Let go. This place is only draining you of your peace. You do not belong here any longer."

"How do you know? You're still here. Is your magic limited to not doing what's right?"

"I am preventing *your* magic from doing what is wrong." Aurora raised her hands as a sliver of colors appeared between the trees, expanding into a circle as it swirled like a doorway to an expanse of shadows. "He hears you and shall return if you are not careful. That gate must remain locked."

A clap of thunder reverberated, and a relentless torrent of rain collided with the rushing river. Enid tilted her head to the sky, letting the rain cascade down her face, but her body shifted into a faded silhouette, remaining untouched as a pocket of dryness surrounded her.

Violet light poured from Aurora, causing the door to the unknown crumble into dust.

Facing Aurora, Enid raised her voice. "What's on the other side of that door?"

"A maelstrom of despair." With graceful steps, Aurora moved toward the edge of the water. A hue of lavender enveloped her as her dress billowed along the rocks. "Your brother's actions will incur consequences, Enid. If you refuse to leave, allow me to help you escape into a timeless peace until his time arrives."

"Timeless peace? Isn't that what I'm doing now? I don't hurt, not like I used to, and time doesn't feel like time at all. I don't even remember what time feels like." The rain soaked the ground, turning the earth to mud as Enid paced back and forth, staying in her dry bubble. "I'm not making sense, am I?"

Aurora smiled. "You know where to find me when you are ready." She vanished, leaving only the faintest echo of her voice in the air.

"I don't know how to find anyone, anymore," Enid said as she stood alone next to the Coda River.

Running along the forest path toward her house, a tolling clock rang in the distance, and she halted on the porch. Never had there been a clock with bells inside. A chill sliced through her as she crossed the threshold in her ghostly form, moving through the door. The ringing subsided, leaving behind a faint echo drowned out by rolling thunder and rain hammering the roof.

"Hello? Anyone home?" Her voice echoed off the walls. "Of course no one is home, no one is ever home anymore..." Clanging reverberated again, but this time laughter joined in. A girl's laughter.

Drew?

A mystical force dragged Enid from her home at Neptune Point, leaving her standing on the doorstep of Maddie Harlow's house. She wasn't sure if Maddie's magic had failed, or if her own magic had worked, but Enid was back.

The night sky brightened into daytime as the sun's rays broke through the clouds. An object near the doormat caught the light, reflecting along the ceramic planters on each side of the door. Enid crouched down, but her fingertips only brushed through a row of stones. As she walked through the doorway, an invisible barrier pushed back, keeping her outside. Either she'd find a way in, or wait until they came outside, but she wasn't leaving until Maddie helped her. Whatever the cost.

Twenty-One

Maddie 2010

Maddie washed paintbrushes in the kitchen sink and laid them on a towel to dry beside the rack of dinner dishes, admiring the stenciled flower art she'd created. She traced her fingers over the vibrant yellows and reds against the sage green cupboards, the paint still slightly tacky beneath her touch. As she poured a cup of tea, the glued chip on the teapot's lid caught her eye. Jack's granddaughter had begged for her help, but she'd shut her away. If her own grand-daughter ever needed help and everyone else abandoned her, Maddie would be heartbroken.

There's nothing I can do for Enid.

As she lifted the mug, chimes on the clock in the other room echoed, and the tea scalded her lips. The heat from the mug blended with a surge of magic in her hands as she entered the den and stood in front of the tall clock. A purple glow shone through the fabric of her shirt, and she tugged the chain, releasing the jewel. The last chime announced seven o'clock and died into the silence as the second hand swept around the clock's face.

Maddie pushed the curtains aside and ran a finger over the crystals on the ledge, but they no longer reacted under her touch. The spell she'd used to keep the dead outside had weakened, and a creeping dread replaced the sense of security she'd had over the past week. Her connection to the magic holding onto the spell thinned like static cutting off a phone call—or resistance from the other side.

Drew's playful chatter drifted from her hideout under the stairs with a mix of giggles and excited whispers. Closing the door to the den, Maddie hurried into the living room and set her mug on the coffee table, heading for the square door at the base of the stairs, just large enough to crawl through.

Drew peeked her head out from under a sea of blankets as a strand of fairy lights cast a glow behind her. "Want to come in with me?"

"Only if I get to know what's so funny." Sitting on a beanbag chair, Maddie pointed at her forehead as she furrowed her brows. "I wouldn't be blessed with these lines if I never got to laugh and cry once in a while."

Drew ran over and climbed on Maddie's lap, holding Maddie's cheeks in her small hands. "You don't have enough lines! You need more laughing, Gran."

"I sure do, darlin'. Give me all you got." Maddie leaned against the cement wall near a round window and wrapped her arms around Drew.

With her hands still on Maddie's cheeks, Drew chewed her lip, watching a butterfly flutter and land on the outside of the windowpane. "If you're my Gran, what would Aiden be?"

Maddie froze, her throat tightening as she held her granddaughter in her arms. Gabe and Joelle used to bring Drew for dinner at Maddie's every few months—that had ended a year ago—but Drew had rarely spoken of her grandfather, other than pointing to a photograph that Maddie still had on the mantle. "Well, I suppose he'd have been Grandad or Grandpa? He would've been happy with whatever you called him."

"What about I call him Fisherman?" Drew asked as the lights sparkled in her curious eyes.

"Aye, his first love, I used to say."

"Before you and Daddy."

"That's right." A shiver ran down Maddie's back as a chill settled around her. Hadn't the spell worked to keep the dead away? "What made you think of your grandfather?"

Drew's hands dropped to her lap, and she looked down. "You'll be mad."

Clasping her hands around Drew's back, Maddie searched her granddaughter's face. "Look at me," she said, and Drew slowly met her gaze. "I could never be mad at you, not ever."

"What if I do something bad?"

"I might feel angry or frustrated, but then we talk about it."

Running a hand over her ponytail, Drew tugged the ends toward her mouth. "Grandpa wants me to tell you he loves you and misses you, and he's happy he met me, and that Daddy will be home again someday and don't worry, and that you're doing a real good job of taking care of me." She covered her mouth with tears in her eyes. "I'm sorry, Gran," she whispered quickly, before holding her breath.

"You see him? Is he here right now?" Maddie's heart pounded against her chest as she struggled to hold back tears.

"I can show you." Drew raised her hands and placed one on Maddie's cheek, and with a deep breath, glancing over her shoulder, extended the other behind her.

A wave of heat washed over Maddie as a sudden light blurred her vision, leaving the sharp taste of copper on her tongue. "What's happening?"

"Hi, love. I just wanted to see you again. She's pretty amazing, isn't she?" Aiden materialized beside Drew, radiating an angelic glow.

Choking back tears, Maddie grasped his hand, lacing her fingers with his. Terrified he'd vanish before she had the chance to tell him, the words spilled out of her. "I love you so much, I miss you."

"So do I." His voice dropped to a ghostly whisper as his silhouette flickered. "It's not safe for her, Mads. You have to make it go away." As he vanished, Drew's hand fell away from Maddie's face, leaving her with the lingering warmth of his touch on her hand.

"Did I do something wrong?" Grabbing a blanket, Drew rubbed her fingers over the satin trim as her lip quivered.

"Not at all, you did a beautiful thing, just beautiful." Maddie cleared the impending tears from her throat and hugged Drew.

She got to see Aiden again and felt the warmth of his smile and his hand in hers. Her granddaughter's abilities could reunite them, bringing him back into her life, but the risk of attracting a powerful, sinister enemy targeting Drew would be too dangerous. Aiden was right. She had to make it go away, all of it.

Setting Drew down, Maddie rose from the beanbag chair. "You need to wash up for bed. First day of school in the morning. Maria's going to pick you up and drop you off with Nico and Simon."

Drew held the blanket in a tight grip as she ducked out of the crawlspace, following Maddie up the stairs to the bathroom. Standing on a stool, she brushed her teeth and washed her face, handing Maddie the facecloth when she was done.

As she combed through the tangles in Drew's hair, her granddaughter observed their reflections in the mirror. "I'm sorry if I made you sad," Drew said.

"I'm not sad, does this look sad?" Maddie scrunched her face and pointed at her forehead. "See? Did I get new lines? It's the happiness coming through, just like I told you."

A smile lit up Drew's face, and Maddie touched her granddaughter's freckled nose. "Look at the gorgeous glitter across your cheeks. They're called *Bricini*, and to have them is magic, did you know that?"

Drew tilted her head, and her hair fell over her face as she scrutinized herself in the mirror. "I'm magic?"

"You sure are. You bring all the magic to my life, darlin'." Maddie embraced her, helping her off the stool and leading her to her bedroom. Turning on the bedside lamp, she tucked her into bed. "I love you, sleep tight."

"The music box?"

Maddie handed Drew the little jewelry box, and she opened the lid, letting the ballerina spin around to the melody. "Night, Gran."

The soft click of Drew's bedroom door echoed in the hallway as Maddie closed it and headed into her room. Her granddaughter would grow up in a world without the dead interfering—even if it meant she never experienced Aiden's presence again. She vowed to give Drew a normal childhood filled with friendships and love, but the only way to do that was through magic one last time.

She retrieved the amulet from its velvet-lined home at the bottom of her jewelry box and rummaged in her closet for the spell book. Descending the stairs, she settled outside on the porch swing, placing the amulet over the book, and sat back against the cushion. The sunset turned the sky pink, and the sea air rustled the leaves, carrying a hint of bonfire smoke from the beach.

The temperature plummeted, the air turning crisp and chilling her skin. A knowing pricked the back of her neck, and she bolted upright. The protection spell had broken, and the dead girl had found her way back. A raven soared across the road with a throaty call, landing on the bare branches of her lilac bushes. She opened the book and held the silver chain in her fingers as the black stone came to life with a spinning thread of light inside the core.

"I told you I can't help you, this has to end." Maddie inhaled, awakening her magic from its slumber. "I'm sorry, Enid."

A warm current flowed through her, casting light from her hands as she held them over the book. "I need a spell to get rid of her gifts... and mine. Forever."

Twenty-Two

Enid 2010

The towering oaks and pine trees surrounding Portal Park at the center of Atlas Cliffs offered shade over the swing set. Sitting beside an oblivious Maddie Harlow on a park bench, Enid closed her eyes, recalling a memory of what the world around her smelled like, conjuring what she could from memory, inhaling the sweet scent of pine and earth as she crossed her feet at her ankles and re-crossed them. She'd gotten good at focusing on becoming more human. It wouldn't be long before the leaves turned gold and red, falling off the branches as snow fell, and the sandbox and swings would hang empty. But days, months, and years all passed the same, like sand through a tiny hole in an hourglass.

Drew shoveled sand into a bucket as a little boy amused himself with a rubber duck on the wooden ledge of the sandbox. With the spell book open on her lap, Maddie held her hands over a blank page, the amulet's light shining from beneath her shirt. Enid glanced over her shoulder, following Maddie's gaze, but no one was there.

I need the amulet back if I'm going to break through her spells.

Giving the amulet back to Maddie was supposed to have been a way to get her attention, not to end up stuck sitting on a park bench, wanting to scream into the void. Maddie had found a way to use the mystical jewel against her, and now Enid's presence went unseen all over again. Every moment that Ben existed as part of the living world was a cruel injustice, igniting a simmering rage inside of her. She could almost see his disgusting, wicked grin as he lived his victorious life somewhere. He'd gotten away with murder, and she couldn't let it go.

Drew burst into laughter, and the boy in the sandbox scowled at her. "What's so funny?" Maddie's gaze remained fixed on the book as she spoke.

"This boy thinks he's in a bathtub with his toy, he doesn't believe me that we're in a park, in sand, like on a beach." Drew tumbled backward from the sandbox, landing on the grass, but Maddie didn't crack a smile.

"There's no one there," Maddie whispered.

"The girl still *sees*." Enid stood from the bench and crouched near the boy. "He's dead, like me."

A serious expression settled on Drew's face as she sat up and brushed strands of red hair out of her wide eyes. "You're back," she said.

"I can't go anywhere without your help..." Enid sighed. "But you're just a kid and can't do a goddamn thing."

"Goddamn?" Drew said.

"Drew Harlow, language." Maddie stood and closed the book, sticking it into an oversized quilted bag as she glanced around and moved closer to the sandbox. "Who are you talking to?"

"I told you, a boy with a toy duck." Drew slowly shifted her gaze from Enid and waved to the boy as he disappeared with a smile, taking the yellow toy with him.

"Goddamn is right." Maddie pursed her lips and scanned the playground.

"Language, Gran."

Now it was Enid's turn to burst into laughter. "So what? She sees me now, but you can't hear me anymore?" She stood next to Maddie with her arms crossed. "What kind of magic are you using?"

Dark clouds rolled in, heavy with the promise of rain, obscuring the sun and casting long shadows. Maddie threaded her hair into a braid, securing it with an elastic from around her wrist. Drew's eyes flickered from Enid to her grandmother.

"Maybe you can tell your grandmother that the lighthouse girl is back." Enid tapped her fingers on her chin as Drew looked at her with a blank stare on her face. "You know the lighthouse? It's like a historical landmark in this town. How can you not know that place? You of all people should know it."

"I'm only five." The pink restored in Drew's lip as she released the hold her teeth had on it. "The lighthouse place?" She immediately resumed chewing on her bottom lip.

The afterlife hadn't given Enid the gift of patience. She was lashing out at a five-year-old, who had enough going on with no parents and seeing dead people.

"Someone's here with you, aren't they?" Maddie held up a raincoat, and Drew stuck her arms in the sleeves.

Drew nodded her head and zipped her jacket before shoving her hands into the pockets. "Did I do something wrong?"

Maddie rubbed her temples. "No, you didn't," she said, dropping her hands to her sides in exasperation. "What about the lighthouse place?"

Drew kicked pebbles with her rubber boots. "That's where she lived."

"Enid," Maddie said.

"She knows exactly who did this to me," Enid blurted. The weight of her situation pressed down on her, pulling her to a breaking point, and it mattered less and less that the only person capable of listening to her was a child.

Drew's lip quivered, and she took to gnawing it raw again. "She maybe died at the lighthouse place."

Shutting her eyes, Maddie took a deep breath. Kneeling at Drew's level, her gaze softened. "I'm going to take you there, just one time. I will show you the lighthouse place, and you will never go back again. And the girl will leave you alone forever, okay? They'll leave you alone from now on, I give you my word." Maddie embraced Drew. Her arms reached around, hugging her grandmother as tears trickled over her flushed cheeks.

Enid followed them as Maddie clasped Drew's hand, leading her back to the car. "You can go out there, but you won't find anything. Go talk to the police and tell them Ben Morana murdered us. Me and my little brother, that's what you need to do! And if you refuse to help me, give back the necklace."

Drew's jaw dropped, and she stared at Enid with fear in her eyes. "What necklace? Gran, she wants her necklace." She yanked her hand away as her grandmother opened the car door.

How could Maddie still have the magic jewel around her neck, but not see me anymore?

The rain intensified, pinging a metallic rhythm off the car. "Just get in, darlin', I'll talk to her."

"But you can't—" Enid said, folding her arms across her chest.

Shutting the car door, Maddie spun around so her back was to Drew. "I know you're still here and she can see you, but she can't help you and neither can I."

Moving closer, Enid extended her hand toward Maddie. "If you won't help, I want Aurora's amulet back. It belongs to me."

"I can't hear you, but I can feel that cold air that always comes." Rubbing her arms, Maddie paced back and forth. "I tried to find him, your brother, but he doesn't exist, not anywhere. There's nothing that says he's still alive at all, and I've been in this world of magic before. I lost my husband because of what I am." Maddie pointed to the rain-streaked car window and Drew looked up at Enid from the other side of the glass. "She'll be a target if that darkness ever returns, and I won't let that happen. Whatever spell I did the other night worked. I can't see or hear you, but I need to make sure I give the same gift to my granddaughter."

"What? *No*. Don't you see? What she already has is a gift." Enid placed her hands on her head, mirroring Maddie's frantic pacing. "No one's going to hurt her, I sure won't. Please don't do this, Maddie."

"I'll return the amulet, the books... I'll bring it all back and put it in the attic where Jack kept it safe." Maddie crossed the front of the car to the driver's side. Gripping the handle, she angled her head out of Drew's line of sight. "I'm sorry for what happened to you and your brother, but we can't be part of this ever again." Collapsing against the seat, she brushed wet hair off her forehead as she started the car and drove away.

A deep ache of hopelessness, cold and heavy, sank through Enid's body. Her fingers grazed over her arm, finding nothing but air as her body shifted into a shimmering ghost against the dark clouds.

Closing her eyes, Enid focused on the lighthouse, and relived memories of home with Blythe and Ezra; her mom and dad gathered around a big holiday dinner with a Christmas tree sparkling in the corner of the living room, and a crackling fire in the fireplace. Ben was nowhere in sight. He often retreated to his bedroom, or the basement tunnels that had always terrified Enid.

When she opened her eyes, she was standing on the front porch of the boarded-up house. Her house. Her empty, devoid of life house. This was home now, and it would have to do. Because a nagging instinct told her she would be stuck here for a while.

The raven landed on the railing beside her, echoing a deep, throaty croak through the stillness. With a slow, careful movement, she offered her hand, and the raven lowered its head, allowing her to brush her fingertips over sleek feathers. "I think you're my only friend here."

Twenty-Three

Maddie 2010

Running toward the waves at Jupiter Cove Beach, Drew and Nico dug holes in the sand, letting the water fill them as they splashed and stomped in the surf. A scattering of locals populated the beach, but they'd kept Jupiter Cove a secret from the tourists with private property signs warning people to stay away. And with school back in session, most had returned to their regular lives away from Atlas Cliffs until the changing leaves in autumn brought them back.

The folding lawn chair shifted in the sand beneath her as Maddie scanned the beach, making sure no one was too close. Lost in their own world, Drew and Nico's laughter carried over the whining seagulls twenty feet away from Maddie. She reached into her beach bag, taking the amulet from the inner pocket, and retrieving the spell book. As she opened the book, the forest scene on the inside cover transformed. The menacing shadow among the trees vanished, replaced by a sliver of rainbow colors.

The door where darkness lives.

Maddie draped the silver chain over her head and her fingers wrapped around the jewel as a thread of light spun in the center. Drew shrieked as she chased a seagull away from Nico's sandcastle, and Maddie's breath caught. She scanned the beach for onlookers, and turned to a blank page, calling on the magic flowing underneath the surface of her skin.

"I need a spell to keep the dead away, no matter the cost," she whispered.

If the door opened, unleashing the darkness where Aiden's killer lurked, Drew would become a target, and without Aurora's help, Maddie would be powerless to send the threatening force away again. Her only choice was to give Drew a normal life, with a regular existence, closing the veil between the living and the dead from Drew's eyes forever.

"Why do I feel so guilty, like I'm stealing her soul?" she muttered under her breath.

"Because you are." Enid's voice brushed against her ear, unseen.

Maddie angled her head down to hide her moving lips as she spoke. "I thought I wouldn't hear you again."

"You should be proud of yourself. Whatever you're doing is keeping me away from you, but please don't do this, Maddie. Don't take away my one hope for peace."

Enid's desperate voice was strained, wavering between close and growing far away. Maddie ached for her, but she had to make a choice, and protecting Drew would always win.

"You'll find peace again, and you won't need us to do it."

"What about your gifts?" Enid's soft voice faded. "I still have magic too, and I know what you're able to do. You bring people back from death, Maddie. What if you need it for her?"

Maddie watched Drew sitting on the beach, scooping up piles of wet sand into the bucket. The dead girl was getting too close, learning too much. The raven's familiar call returned, and seagulls scattered as it landed on a piece of driftwood nearby. A chill crawled down her back, and tingling swirled along her jaw as a metallic taste pricked her tongue with a sharp, cooling sensation. The page in the book lifted, floating back down as purple lettering danced over the opposite page. The shimmering letters settled into sentences, and a vibrant glow behind the words dimmed.

What you lose will come back again.

Another cascade of glittering letters crawled along the page.

Woven shield of protection, thicken the veil, binding her sight...

"What's that book?" Drew pushed wet strands of hair away from her eyes as she sprinted toward the lawn chair covered in sand, and Maddie snapped it shut, stuffing it back inside the bag.

"Nothing, darlin'. Are you ready to go home?"

"We want the boards," Drew said, breathless.

Nico trailed behind her with sand clinging to his legs and face. "Can we take them?"

"Can we, please?" Drew's eyes reflected the sunlight, displaying a jade-green shade like her dad's and Aiden's.

The tide rolled in with small waves crashing over the shoreline, but Maddie found no gaps between the waves showing an undertow, and the kids had swum with the boogie boards Nico's father had bought for them all summer. She stood, handing them each a board and followed Drew and Nico near the edge of the water as they charged into the small waves curling toward shore like they belonged in the ocean. "You know the rules, stay close, make sure—"

"My feet *are* touching." Gripping her board, Drew jumped over a wave, kicking her feet out.

Tying her sundress in a knot at her side, Maddie waded into the frigid water. Wind blew off the surface of the water, tousling her hair, and numbness spread from her feet to her calves, but she refused to leave the water until the kids were done.

The book gave her a spell, but would the magic work?

What you lose will come back again.

Would Drew's ability to see the dead return some day? But what about the Sisterhood's protection? Ending the mystic cycle would eliminate the need for protection.

Nico sat on his boogie board as Drew shielded her eyes, focusing on a strange rogue wave steamrolling toward shore, and Maddie trudged deeper until the water reached her knees. "Drew, come back here, you're going too far!"

"Wave, Drew! It's too big!" Nico screamed.

The wave surged over Drew, tossing her from her board and swirling her fiery red hair under the churning water. A rush of blood drained from Maddie's head to her frozen legs as she released a tortured scream. "Drew!" The wave crashed into Maddie, pulling her under before she could react. She burst through the surface, gasping for air, spinning around in the water, searching for her granddaughter. She couldn't lose her—she'd never be able to live with herself. The world surrounding her blurred as she moved in uncoordinated chaos. Water slapped at her face, stinging her eyes, the current pulling at her legs. "Drew!"

"There she is!" Nico slid off his board, swimming past Maddie's legs.

Holding her breath, Maddie dove under, staying close to him. Although the shore was close, she felt adrift in the middle of the ocean. Panic rose in her chest, but fierce determination propelled her forward with a rush of adrenaline. Tethered to her neck, the amulet glowed, floating in the water. Diving beneath the surface, she opened her eyes as light streamed from the jewel, shaped like a hand, reaching for Drew's submerged face.

Nico reached Drew first, turning her on her back as he lifted her face out of the water. "Maddie, help!"

"I'm here." Waves pushed them toward shore as Maddie held Drew's head above the water, dragging Nico with her arm around his waist. "Drew, can you hear me?" Maddie called as a few people gathered on shore to help. Drew's lips turned blue, and her face paled.

Zane Salinger appeared, wading in the water, taking Nico from her grasp as she lay Drew onto the sand and hovered over her. People surrounded them, offering their assistance. Maddie positioned her hands for CPR, but Zane gestured for them to give her space and ordered someone to call for help.

But as Maddie summoned her magic, the frantic cries surrounding her faded, replaced by a soft, warm glow pouring from her hands and flowing into her granddaughter's chest.

Breathe life.

With her back to the small crowd blocking their view, Maddie leaned over and unleashed a torrent of magical power. Sand swirled in a powerful gust of wind, forcing the small group who'd gathered to cover their faces. Clouds moved in, blocking the sun, and the air stilled as Drew's chest finally rose and fell in a quick burst. Water emerged from her throat in choked gurgles as Maddie turned her onto her side.

Coughing up water and gasping for air, sobs racked Drew's chest, and her body trembled, but the pink returned to her skin and lips. Maddie scooped her up into her arms with her hand on the back of her crying granddaughter's head. "I'm so sorry, oh my God." Salt water and tears streamed down Maddie's face as she held Drew. "Look at me, love." She held Drew's cheeks in her hands and kissed her forehead. "Deep breaths."

Drew breathed in and hyperventilated through tears, exhaling in a fit of coughing, and Nico threw his arms around her. "Is she hurt?" Wet hair stuck to his forehead, and he wiped dripping water from his face.

"She'll be all right. You did good, Nico, you're a hero." Maddie lost feeling in her arms as she clung to Drew, unable to let her go until she knew for sure she wouldn't die. People who'd flocked to their sides dispersed as Zane talked to them, glancing back at Maddie with furrowed brows. "Nico, can you run and grab towels?" she said through her own tears.

"The boards..." Nico pointed at the water as the two small boards floated away from shore.

"I'll get them." Zane patted Maddie on the shoulder as he hurried to the water, wading in to retrieve both boards.

Nico rushed back from the lawn chair with towels, and Drew squirmed out of Maddie's arms, wiping her nose with the towel he gave her as she wrapped it around herself.

Folding the lawn chair, Zane draped Maddie's bag over his shoulder and trudged through the sand toward her.

"Thanks, here, let me take something." She reached for the bag on his shoulder, and he shrugged it off, handing it to her as he adjusted the boards and chair in his arms. Rummaging through the bag, she found a sweater and draped it over Drew's shivering body. Drew stuck her wet arms in the sleeves, and Maddie secured the towel around her granddaughter's waist. "Are you okay?"

"Yeah, I wanna go home." Drew slipped her feet into bright pink flip-flops and headed for the stone steps, sniffling. Nico caught up to her, talking to her as he stayed close to her side.

Lines surrounded Zane's blue eyes as they flickered past Maddie. "That wave came out of nowhere, it was weird. She seems okay..." He glanced back at her, concern etched across his forehead. "Are you?"

"I'm fine." The waves had calmed as the tide crept up the beach, leaving a trail of wet sand speckled with raindrops. Had something more than a rogue wave swept Drew underwater? Cold air brushed her face, making her breath visible, despite the warmth of the early evening.

Zane's defined jaw twitched as he observed her, but he maintained his stoic expression. "I'll carry these, if you can grab my stuff over there."

Drew and Nico had almost reached the top of the steps leading to the road, and Maddie yelled for them to wait as she grabbed Zane's things. Shaking sand from his towel, she noted the Sloan Enterprises logo embroidered on the corner and recalled the conversation with Maria about Nico's dad. Zane jogged to catch up to the kids, and Maddie hurried behind him. "You do business with them?"

"Who?" Zane asked, pausing on the first step.

She pointed to the towel embroidery and rushed past him, motioning for Drew and Nico to cross the road as cars drove away and people stared, talking amongst themselves.

"Not me, but my son has been talking to them. He won't listen to me; I don't like the guy running the show over there. Why, you know him?"

"I knew his mother-in-law. They seem to be offering a lot of help in town," Maddie said.

"And he wants everyone to know it like he's some sort of king. I just don't trust him, but I'm probably jaded, and my bullshit detector has gotten good." A mischievous glint appeared in Zane's eyes as he smiled.

"Can't argue with that." Maddie handed Zane his stuff and carried the boogie boards and lawn chair up the driveway toward the shed.

"What kind of car is this?" Nico cupped his hands around his face, peering inside the window of a sleek blue car parked along the side of the road near her driveway. Zane unlocked the car, opening the back door.

"Hands off, Nico—" Maddie's voice echoed in the quiet shed as she placed the boards and chair inside. The towel lay crumpled on the porch and the sweater Drew wore hung over her knees as she ran around picking dandelions off the front yard. A mist of rain hung in the air, birds chirped, hidden in the lilac bushes lining the side of the house, and nothing sinister lurked, but a tension of unseen eyes on her gave Maddie an unnerving feeling they weren't alone. Locking the shed, she headed back down the driveway.

"It's a Mustang... 1973. Took me months to restore it and she'll go into storage soon, but it's a classic." Zane dropped his towel on the floor of the back seat as he showed Nico the dash of the car.

"I want a car just like this." Nico's face beamed.

As Maddie approached Zane, her eyes locked on his, and a nervous flutter danced in her stomach, giving way to guilt over her reaction to him. "Come on, Nico, your mom will be here soon to pick you up, run inside and change."

"Can Drew come to my house for dinner?"

"Another night, okay?" She tousled his dark hair as he charged barefoot up the driveway into the house.

Maddie undid the knot in her soaking wet dress, letting it fall to her ankles as she ran her fingers through her tangled mess of damp hair. "Thanks for your help today. I still don't know what happened, I had my eyes on her the whole time... When she went under, I—" Maddie looked away, rubbing her arms as tears threatened to fall.

Shutting the back door, Zane moved until he was inches from Maddie, and she fought an urge to wrap her arms around him and feel his warmth against her skin.

I've got a child to raise, and problems no one can possibly understand... and I still love my husband.

A crushing weight settled on her chest as she thought of Aiden. It had been so long since she'd had love in her life like his... So very long.

"Is this you being fine again?" The charming crinkle appeared around Zane's blue eyes again.

"How'd you know?"

"Good instincts, I guess." Rain intensified, and he ran a hand through his hair.

"It's raining, Gran!" Drew yelled from the porch as she ran inside, letting the screen door slam behind her.

"I've got to go." Maddie shifted her stance, turning away from him.

"Dinner sometime?" Zane opened the driver's side door, hovering over the door frame. "Sorry, let me try that again. Will you have dinner with me sometime?"

"You seem like a nice man..."

A really nice, kind, attractive man.

She took a deep breath. "Look, I'm not just babysitting here, she lives with me. My son's gone for months—"

"My schedule is non-existent, Maddie. I'll adjust it to what works for you, no pressure at all. I'd just like to see you, have conversations, watch a sunset or something. That's all." He hunched over inside the car and grabbed something, emerging with a pen in hand and scribbled on a scrap of paper, handing it to her. "Here's my number, use it anytime. I'm a sucker for last minute, no plans. Whenever the mood hits, say the word and I'll be there."

Before she could come up with another excuse to keep him away, her lips curled into a tight smile. "Okay, I could do that."

"I look forward to it." He sat in the car with a grin and started the engine, waving as he drove away.

The front door opened, and Drew peeked her head outside. "Can we have a cookie?"

"It's too close to dinnertime," Maddie said. The amulet pulsed warmth along her neck, and she folded the paper from Zane, grasping the jewel as a burst of sparkling light cascaded inside it. For the first time since the mystical stone had entered her life, she had forgotten it existed. She clung to a glimmer of hope that a *normal* life without magic was possible for both herself and Drew.

Twenty-Four

Maddie 2010

Steam filled the bathroom as Maddie emerged from the shower and dried off. She dressed in a soft pajama set and ran a brush through her wet hair, shaking out the loose strands with her fingers. The hum of chatter echoed on the other side of the door, and she opened it a crack. Drew's hushed voice carried from her bedroom to the hallway, and Maddie froze, straining to make out what she was saying. The moment

Drew fell asleep, Maddie would do what needed to be done to remove her granddaughter's connection to the other side.

A spark flickered deep inside the amulet as it rested on the counter and she picked up the silver chain, draping it over her head. Lifting the jewel, electricity surged along her fingers, settling in her palm, and a draft of icy air curled around her face. Letters materialized in the condensation over the mirror's surface and a message appeared.

She means no harm.

"Doesn't matter," Maddie muttered as the inscription disappeared and another message took its place.

What she loses shall return.

Snatching a towel, she wiped away the message from the mirror and tossed it into the hamper. "Go away, leave us alone."

She concealed the jewel underneath her shirt and flipped the light switch, plunging the bathroom into darkness before heading to Drew's room.

Sitting on the window bench, Drew snapped the music box closed, and its sweet melody faded into silence with a high-pitched metallic spring. "Is magic real? The girl is back, and she says so."

"Of course she does." The frigid air returned, encircling Maddie. Fear masked itself as intense anger, flaring in her chest.

Enid was relentless, and Maddie had reached her breaking point.

"She told me you see it too."

"See what?" Maddie sat on the edge of the bed.

"The scary shadow who made the water big and pushed me." Drew's gaze drifted toward her vanity in the corner of the room.

The amulet thrummed against Maddie's skin with the beat of her heart, and whispered chatter brushed her ear. She angled her ear against her shoulder to drown out the sound and turned her focus on Drew. This child had no one except Maddie. As much as she loved her son, he'd left his daughter when she needed him most, and Drew's mother proved to be a selfish woman who'd abandoned her for a new life. Welcome to the Sisterhood? More like welcome to motherhood all over again. For as long as Drew needed her, Maddie would provide a safe haven, fulfilling the role of a protective, nurturing parent. She refused to allow anyone dead or alive to hurt her granddaughter.

Standing, Maddie pulled the covers back and patted the bed. "Time for sleep, hop in."

Drew climbed into bed, clutching the music box against her chest. Maddie covered her, tucking the blankets around her and brushed hair away from her forehead. "Remember what I told you about that girl?"

"You'd take care of it." Drew's eyes watered as she yawned.

"That's right. When you wake up tomorrow, it'll be a new day, and she'll be gone."

"But she's nice, what if I miss her?"

"Say your goodbyes now then," Maddie said. The chill in the air swirled between them and their breaths misted. Drew had never mentioned seeing the mist, or feeling the cold when the dead were near, but her eyes widened, following the billows of fog.

"Goodbye, friend," Drew said.

Maddie froze as a lump caught in her throat.

Friend?

Her granddaughter was making *friends* with the dead.

"I hope you get to go somewhere fun and that you see your mom again. Maybe I'll get to see mine too." Tears escaped Drew's eyes, tracing paths down her freckled cheeks.

Maddie wiped her own eyes before tears could fall. Blocking the other side was the only way to keep Drew safe—it was for the best.

"She's still here, Gran."

"I know, darlin', but when you wake up—"

"She'll be gone, I know, you said so." Drew yawned again, her eyes fluttering closed before they snapped open. "Unless I don't go to sleep."

Rising from the bed, Maddie kissed Drew's forehead. "You had a busy day, sleep will make you refreshed for school tomorrow."

"Leave the light on," Drew said.

"Done." She flicked the switch on the night table and left the room, taking a deep breath. The clock's chimes echoed up the stairs with a soft, dreamlike ringing, keeping in time with the amulet's vibrations along her neck. The mellow tones faded into silence as Maddie walked toward her bedroom to retrieve the spell book she'd hidden in her closet.

Closing the door, she hugged the book against her chest. The mattress sank beneath her as she collapsed on the bed. Casting the spell would have consequences, it always did. But the only price she could imagine was a life without magic, and no more wandering souls haunting her granddaughter.

A sudden wave of icy mist swept over her like cobwebs sticking to her skin.

"Don't do this, please." Enid's desperate tone filled her ears.

"I have to—"

"No, you don't! Look what you did today, she would've died if it weren't for your magic."

Maddie flipped the pages, searching for the earlier spell, and light radiated from the amulet. "You were there today, did you push her off her board? Was that you trying to make some kind of point?" She stood and spun around in the room, unable to see the dead girl as misted breaths crossed with her own.

"How dare you accuse me of trying to kill someone! Especially a kid! It's my brother who's a murderer, not me."

The pages of the book turned in a frantic chaos as a thread of light stretched from the amulet. A sharp inhale pulled the air from the room like a vacuum, and the book stilled as its pages fell open to the intricate lettering of the blocking spell. The light shifted into an ancient quill pen, writing on the opposite page.

Maddie hovered over the book and a silver thread materialized along the spine where the pages were bound. The light within the words dimmed, bringing them into focus.

Sever the thread, cutting ties to memories of the dead
Burn these words to embers for no names shall be remembered.
"I'm doing this tonight, Enid."

As she reached for the book, the pressure of fingers encircled her wrist, yanking her hand back. "Please, I'm begging you to stop this. As long as you wear the necklace, you can hear me, right? I promise I won't bother Drew anymore, I give you my word."

Maddie closed her eyes, reciting the blocking spell in the book, and reached her other hand out to where the girl clasped her wrist. "I'm sorry, but this is something I have to do. I can't let her stay connected to a world I can't protect her from, especially after what happened to her today. I hope you find your peace." Releasing her hand, Enid's grip on her wrist faded and the surrounding air warmed.

The candlelight on the bedside table cast an orange glow on Drew's hair, fanned out over the pillow like a halo as she slept. Maddie sat on the bed with the amulet's weight heavy against her neck, and the silver thread between her fingers. "If you ever discover the secrets of what I'm about to do, I hope you'll forgive me."

Ignoring the persistent worry that she was interfering with fate by making a decision that wasn't hers to make, she whispered the spell as tears stung her cheeks. "Woven shield of protection, thicken the veil, binding her sight. May no wandering soul mend the thread, let memories fade like the darkness of night."

She wouldn't take any chances, and if removing Drew's memories of every ghost she'd ever encountered, including Aiden, meant a stronger barrier between the living and the dead, Maddie would leave no stone unturned. With a pair of scissors, she cut the silver thread, and purple light flowed from the amulet, consuming the thread as it fell to the floor. "Sever the thread, cutting ties to memories of the dead." She opened the ripped page of the spell book, revealing the inscribed spells, and held it over the candle, letting the flame consume the yellowed paper. "Burn these words to embers for no names shall be remembered."

The light spun, extinguishing the candle, and swept up the ashes as they floated upward and disappeared.

"What is lost shall return." Aurora's ethereal voice hung in the air, dropping into a deathly stillness.

A shrill ringing buzzed in Maddie's ears, and she gritted her teeth, taking a deep breath. Her head ached, and a flash of pain shot down her body to her feet. She bolted off the bed, and a wave of dizziness slammed into her. Using the dresser to steady herself against a wave of nausea, she breathed in and out slowly. Drew stirred in her sleep, flopping onto her back with a whine, but settled as her fingers gripped the corner of the blanket.

Maddie's stomach lurched violently as bile rose in her throat. Covering her mouth, she stumbled into the bathroom and dropped to the floor, clutching the toilet as she threw up. Uncontrollable shivers racked her body as she hoisted herself up, gripping the edges of the counter with both hands. Her bloodshot eyes stared back at her in the mirror, and she ran the tap, rinsed her mouth, and soaked a facecloth in hot water.

What have I done?

Heat from the cloth burned her skin as she held it against her face, but it eased the numbness that had consumed her when she'd completed the spell. It was as though she grasped for the familiar tether to an existence she'd always known, but it had vanished, leaving her with a hollowed emptiness. The magic that had been a part of her for decades, her power... *Gone.*

As she dropped the cloth in the sink, the amulet caught her eye. The stone was cold under her touch, and an inky black cloud had drowned out the light, plunging it into an unnerving stillness.

Whimpering cries drifted from Drew's bedroom, and Maddie rushed to her side as her eyes fluttered open, revealing agonizing heartache. "I had a bad dream," Drew said.

"What about?"

"I was all alone here, it was scary. Mommy and Daddy were gone too, and I didn't know what to do." Drew sat up and wrapped her arms around Maddie's neck, burying her face as she sobbed.

"It's just a nightmare, it isn't real." Maddie rubbed Drew's back. "I'm not going anywhere. You won't be alone, okay?"

"Promise?"

"I promise." Releasing Drew, Maddie turned off the lamp and crawled under the blankets, laying next to her.

"You'll stay with me, Gran?" Drew placed her hand on Maddie's cheek.

"For as long as you like."

As her granddaughter's breathing settled into a gentle rhythm, Maddie took the amulet off her neck. Moonlight filtered through a gap in the curtains, shining on the darkened jewel. It was lifeless now, becoming a stranger in her hands. The necklace no longer belonged to her—perhaps it never really had.

She ran her fingernails along her palms and arms, but the familiar thrum of magic that had once shimmered over her skin had disappeared. A true test awaited them at the lighthouse. Maddie would go back to Neptune Point one last time, keeping her promise to return the amulet to Enid.

Twenty-Five

Enid 2010

The raven extended its wings and soared through the train, perching on a tree branch near the Keeper's house as Enid stood on the porch. With Drew's excited chatter filling the air, Maddie held her hand, guiding her over the hill, protectively holding onto a canvas bag slung over her shoulder with her other hand.

They'd both come to her house, exactly where she'd wanted them, but neither of them could see or hear her anymore. Witnessing Maddie cast the spell had been the first time Enid felt a sense of pain since she'd died. It had been like a sharp blade slicing through her chest in a fleeting moment of intense agony, ending too fast for her to grasp.

Justice wasn't on her side, not anymore.

Maddie glanced at the front door of the house, but she continued toward the lighthouse. Releasing her hand, Drew stomped in puddles with her rubber boots, laughing as water sprayed into the air.

Enid followed them, waving her arms in front of an oblivious Drew. "Where are you going?"

Maddie's expression appeared stern with her narrowed gaze and pursed lips. "This is the lighthouse. It's part of this town's history, but we're not allowed to come back after today, okay?"

Staring skyward at the rotating beacon, Drew lifted her hand and pointed to a nearby tree. Rain spattered, pinging on the hood of her yellow jacket. "That bird is watching us."

"It's just a bird, come with me." Maddie extended her hand to Drew, who took it with reluctance, keeping her eyes fixed on the raven.

Maddie's pace quickened and Drew stumbled in the sand, gripping her grandmother's hand to avoid falling. But Maddie's focus was back on the house as she rushed up the porch steps, releasing Drew's hand. She grabbed the door handle, but the door wouldn't budge. "Damn door." Maddie's gaze shifted upward, blinking as the rain pelted her face. She glanced over her shoulder at Drew, who plucked a speckled stone from the sand and was dusting it off with her fingers. "Stay close," she ordered.

Kicking the toe of her boot in a muddy footprint, Drew nodded as Maddie opened her bag and grabbed a screwdriver, along with another tool Enid didn't recognize, setting to work on the door hinges.

"Breaking and entering is a crime." Enid leaned against the house, stepping into her human form as Drew hopped up the stairs onto the porch and removed her hood. "You know what else is?" Enid continued. "Murder." They both ignored her. The magic had worked, but she had magic of her own, and the amulet would be hers again.

I'm on my own.

Maddie groaned as she pried the hinges off the door. "Put your hood back up or you'll catch cold."

A sudden defiance crept into the little girl's eyes, and Enid crouched down in front of her. "She doesn't want you to see me, but I'm not scary, and I would never hurt you."

The door creaked open as Maddie let out a holler. "I did it! Come inside out of the rain." She reached behind her for Drew, but she stood with her arms crossed.

"I don't like it here," Drew said.

"Me neither—"

"Why couldn't I be with Nell?"

"Because she's working, so I can do this. It'll be quick. Just come inside, five minutes and we're out of here." Desperation crept into Maddie's voice, and Drew gave in, following her grandmother inside.

"You broke the door open, now what? This is ridiculous." Enid marched to the piano and slammed her hands over the keys, sending a chaotic jarring sound echoing in the grand living room. "Can either of you hear that?"

Maddie headed up the stairs, but Drew yanked her hand away. "I'm not going up." She crossed her arms, and a cloud of dust billowed as she flopped onto a broken chair.

Gripping the bag across her mid-section with both hands, Maddie's eyes darted from the top of the stairs to Drew. "I need you to stay right where you are, got it? Don't move."

Drew swung her boots in circles as she sat, staring at the stairs. "Why are you going up there? What if someone lives there?"

"No one lives here anymore. I have to drop something off, but I'll be back in a flash." Maddie turned away from Drew, and continued up the stairs, hesitating as her gaze fell back on Drew. "Stay."

"Gran, I'm not a dog like Nico has... Damn."

"Language." Maddie pointed at Drew.

Drew's eyes widened as she scanned the staircase. "Four minutes." She held her hand up and tucked her thumb against her palm. "Then you come back."

"That's right, just a few minutes."

"What if I have to pee?"

"Hold it and wait." Bounding up the stairs two at a time, Maddie's breath hitched as she reached the landing.

"The amulet better be in that bag." Enid rushed up the stairs after her and tugged the bag open, peering inside, but Maddie didn't move. "You must be so proud of yourself, using magic to steal hers away, leaving me alone with a killer who gets to be free. First rule of being a witch, Maddie Harlow, don't cause *harm*." Something flickered at the edge of Enid's mind as a memory materialized of her and Celeste upstairs in her bedroom reading everything they could find about witches, mystics and magic spells, the curse of the Neptune Point lighthouse, and talismans.

The amulet.

"The amulet shall belong to her when the time is right." Aurora stood near the banister at the top of the staircase in a purple haze.

"You keep talking about time this and time that, but time isn't doing anything for me, not at this time anyway." Shifting into a ghostly silhouette, Enid approached Aurora. "Her gift is gone, she can't see me anymore. It's over."

"They are part of the Sisterhood, as are we, and that shall never be over." Wisps of smoke curled from Aurora's gown as she glided along the hallway, following Maddie. "This woman and her granddaughter are mystics—"

"Witches, we're witches."

"We are blessed with gifts to heal. We possess the light among the darkness and magic to breathe life into the world surrounding us. Forgive me, child, but women were murdered for using such a label where I come from."

Enid held her hands up and they shimmered with their own light, casting sparkles along the floor. "How do you think I got here?" Her voice wavered, startling her.

"I see. I am truly sorry." Aurora placed a hand on Enid's cheek and warmth cascaded through her, wrapping her in an embrace. "Justice shall seek and find him. Of that, I am sure. Blocking magic never holds forever, the fates will intervene. Trust me." She rounded the corner into the last bedroom after Maddie, and Enid moved through the wall to join her.

Maddie dropped her bag on the floor and retrieved a pocket watch. She opened the gold face, snapping it shut and dropping it inside a box on the dresser coated in a layer of dust. "This is yours, Jack. Take care, wherever you are."

"She's bringing it all back, everything my grandfather gave her," Enid said, following Maddie up the attic stairs in the closet. "I don't get it. If you're as powerful as you are, why not step in and help me? Why don't you cast a spell of your own and make all this stop, show yourself to them, too."

Without using the stairs, Aurora appeared in the attic. Her dark eyes watched Maddie as she left the stack of books in a pile behind a large trunk. "Revealing myself to the child would only cause fear. Her soul is not ready for what is to come. Not yet."

Maddie pulled the necklace over her head and kissed the amulet, tucking it inside the spell book. "I don't know if you're here, but this belongs to you now. I hope you find peace." Wiping her eyes, she ran out of the attic and down the stairs, her footsteps thundering into the distance as her trembling voice called out to Drew.

Enid opened the spell book and picked up the amulet as the slam of a door echoed from downstairs. "They're gone."

"They are, and you can leave as well. Let me help you, Enid, as I have done for Ezra and your mother."

I'm not leaving, I'll wait her out. Drew Harlow is the grand-daughter of a witch. She will see me again.

"No, I'm not ready."

Aurora raised a blistered hand and pointed at the amulet around Enid's neck. "Take care of the power within. If used incorrectly, you could open a door that should never be un-locked."

A strange sensation pricked in Enid's chest as Aurora dis-solved into a purple mist. It was as though her lungs needed breaths that never came, and her hands reached for a lifeline that no one gave her. She felt like there was a weight on her shoulders, but also like she was free-falling, with no connec-tion to the living or the dead.

Aurora had offered her a way out, but Enid had the amulet back in her hands, and a magic spell book. She was a witch. Power still clung to her soul, and she wasn't giving up... Not yet.

Maddie 2010

Winter's icy grip settled on Atlas Cliffs, leaving the once vibrant trees bare. Without magic to save them, Maddie's flowers had long wilted under frost and snow. Peace had followed the loss of her magic, but a subtle ache in her chest yearned for a small glimmer of who she used to be.

The door chimes rang consistently, fading into background noise at the Tough Cookie. Tourists no longer busied the town, but with Christmas around the corner, the bakery was as busy as the summer months with festive orders of cookies and desserts for holiday parties. When the last customers left for the day, Maddie flipped the sign to 'closed', locking the front door of the shop.

The swinging door opened, and Nellie carried a stack of clean plates, placing them in the cupboard behind the counter. "Did you hear Nico is buying Drew a surfboard with his own money for her birthday?" She glanced over her shoulder with eyebrows raised and an amused smile. "Those two are adorable, Mads. They're like little soulmates who'll be friends till the end of time."

"A January birthday is too cold, and I'm not letting her in the water on a board of any kind until I'm sure she can handle it," Maddie said, shaking her head. Without magic to save Drew from death, her need to protect her granddaughter had heightened. "And soulmates only exist in fairy tales."

"Whatever, says the woman who is dating a man who treats her like gold."

Zane had signed up for dance classes with her, he'd taken her to dinner many times, and made her birthday tolerable for the first time since Aiden had died. The back of her neck tightened, moving into her chest as a sudden longing for her husband stole the air from her lungs. "He's a friend, I lost my soulmate a long time ago."

Nellie's hands dropped to her sides and her eyebrows knitted together. "Oh, Maddie, I didn't mean it like that, the words come out without a check-in with my brain sometimes—"

"It's not you, it's me. I guess some things are harder to let go of, that's all." Maddie gave her a quick squeeze and untied her apron, draping it over her arm. "Zane is a great guy, and I love spending time with him. I just don't want to let myself get too close, not with Drew at home, now."

"You're allowed to have a boyfriend and bring him home." Nellie held the door open, and Maddie trailed her into the kitchen. "Hell, what if it got serious, and you talked marriage or something? Then what?"

"Then nothing, I'm not getting married again." Maddie hung up the apron and grabbed her purse from the small office down the hall. Drew was her priority and always would be.

Nellie flipped the lights off and shrugged her long coat on, tucking her short hair underneath a knit hat. "Drew is an easygoing kid, and he's great with her. I just don't want you to miss out on something amazing because you're too stuck in your own head."

"I'll always be too stuck in my own head." Maddie laughed, shutting the heavy door as they stepped outside into the parking lot. "Her mother chose another man over her own daughter, and Gabe is saying now he might not make it home for the holidays—he had a bike shipped and it was Nico who taught her to ride it in their garage." Anger rose in her chest, and she took a deep breath, inhaling the crisp evening air. "I adore Zane, but she comes first, Nell."

Nellie unlocked her car and dropped her purse inside. "She's lucky to have you."

"I'm the lucky one. She keeps things light, as strange as that sounds... I love her like she's my own daughter."

"You're her haven, that's what I call it anyway. And I know I've got my own family with Jess and Zach, but this place... It's that home feeling, you know?" A rush of air swirled snow across the parking lot, and Nellie shivered, climbing into her car with. "Okay, let's get out of here. Don't you have a tree to decorate tonight?"

"Yes, yes I do." With a wave over her shoulder, Maddie turned toward her car as Nellie drove away. A streetlight flickered, and the snow sparkled near the back step. Crouching, she picked up a black crystal she'd placed at the back door months earlier, wiping it off. Closing her eyes, she held it in her hand, summoning the magic as she sometimes did—a ritual to reassure herself it hadn't returned. There was no shift or crackle in the air, no electricity coursing through her, no tingling underneath her skin. And the rhythmic splashing of slush under car tires and a distant siren wailing were the only sounds breaking the evening's silence.

She should be grateful for securing Drew's safety, blocking her from those lurking on the other side, but Aiden's death would forever haunt her. What she couldn't confess to Nellie was that adjusting to a new life without magic hadn't been as easy as she'd thought it would be. She had to discover what made her special to the world now and accept a new normal. Drew had given Maddie purpose. When her granddaughter had first come to live with her, she didn't believe she could raise a child again, but Drew was her glimmer, her reason to smile. And those lines on her face were better than any frown lines.

She tossed the stone in the air and caught it, tucking the cold rock in her pocket.

I've got a Christmas tree to decorate.

Leaving downtown behind, she headed along the coastal road to pick Drew up from Maria's.

With a soft glow, the colorful lights sparkled like glitter on the tree. Glass ornaments reflected the light from the fire as flames warmed the room. Maddie sat in her chair with a glass of red wine, and Drew watched a holiday cartoon on television.

Yawning, Drew stretched out her legs, pulling the knitted blanket over herself from the back of the sofa. "That reindeer looks like the same one on my shirt." She pointed to the front of her pajamas.

"It sure does," Maddie said, rocking her chair. "Bedtime once this is over."

"One more? No school tomorrow."

"But you're coming with me to work until Maria can pick you up, so we've got to get up early."

With a sigh, her arms flopped to her sides, and she peered at Maddie over the armrest, her eyes half-closed. "Can I bake with Nellie for the people?"

A laugh escaped Maddie, and she placed her glass on the side table as the show ended on the screen. "You can bake with Nellie for the people any day."

Following Drew upstairs to her bedroom, she tucked her in, handed her the music box, and turned on the lamp. As she headed for the door, Drew muttered something, and she turned around. "What'd you say, darlin'?"

"Nothing." Laying on her side, Drew opened the music box and wound the tiny metal handle to start the melody, but her gaze was on the window bench.

A sinking feeling gripped Maddie, and she moved near the window, pulling the curtains tighter. There was no chill in the air and nothing had changed.

It's in my head, she's just being a kid.

"Goodnight," she said, kissing Drew's forehead and tousling her hair.

"'Night." Drew rubbed her eyes and yawned.

As Maddie left the room, the music box slipped from Drew's hands to her side, and she drifted off to sleep.

Maddie picked up her wineglass and headed into the den. The chimes on the clock hadn't made a sound since her magic disappeared, remaining frozen. Tapping the glass, she stood back and waited, but the hands on the clock kept regular time, sweeping around the ornate face. The jarring clang of the phone startled her, and she reached for it as her heart pounded against her chest.

"Hello?"

"Hi Maddie, it's Zane."

A smile touched her lips, and she sat on the edge of the desk. Heat flushed her neck and cheeks as she talked with him. He asked about her day, and Drew. Perhaps Nellie was right, but she liked how things were with him. Simple, comfortable, and without expectations.

She had no idea what else life held for her, Gabe and Drew, or if Drew's mom would return, reclaiming her daughter, but a fragile hope bloomed in Maddie's chest. The pain of losing Aiden would forever be a part of her, but she also knew she'd see him again one day, and until that time came, she'd never stop loving him.

Twenty-Seven

Enid 2010

The ocean slammed against the rocks, hurling sea spray mixing with snow into the air that Enid would never feel on her living self again. The blizzard swirled around her, as though a giant snow globe held her captive, but untouched by the cold and ice. She remembered her last holiday alive, gathered around the fireplace with lights from the tree lighting up the living room. If she shut her eyes, she could still smell the turkey roasting in the oven and taste the cinnamon and sugar from the apple pie on her tongue. But out here, in a middle of nowhere existence, she'd all but given up.

Her fingers tightened around the amulet as the silver chain dangled over her hand, swaying in the wind, but she couldn't feel the silver edges cutting into her palm. Magic had failed her. The amulet and spell book proved useless against the invisible barrier that surrounded her. The calm she'd once had in Drew's presence, knowing she had been seen—really *seen* and heard—had vanished, leaving her with a silent scream, trapped inside her with a strange, agonizing pressure building against her chest, with no way to unleash the madness.

I can't live like a dead girl anymore.

The light inside the amulet intensified, spinning faster and faster as she lifted the chain, letting it dangle as she stepped onto the rocky edge overlooking the churning sea.

"What are you doing with that?" Pointing to the necklace, Ezra appeared beside her.

"It doesn't work anymore, Ez. Nothing I do works anymore." As a surge of water rolled over the rocks, she clutched the amulet back in her hand, flinging it into the air as the wave swallowed it.

Ezra reached his hand out to her. "You got rid of it, Enid. It's time to go, don't you hear that?" His voice grew distant as his silhouette blurred.

She heard nothing other than the thunderous ocean's constant roar. Her soul wouldn't let her join Ezra, not until Ben got what he deserved. Hugging him, she whispered in his ear. "You go, it's not my time."

A sly smile spread across his angelic face. "I'll be back when it is." An older tone resonated in his voice as he vanished into a fine mist, leaving her standing alone.

She'd become used to loneliness, settling into a solo life where the days and nights blended and time stood still, but also passed faster than she could understand. Her soul would wander until the truth was dug up from wherever it was buried, breaking the chains that held her in between life and death.

Stepping down from the boulder, she approached her house as a car zoomed around the corner, sliding across the road and coming to a halting stop at the top of the hill. A woman got out and slammed the door, pulling her hat down over her ears, and the hood of her oversized parka over her head as she ran down the hill, slipping and tumbling into the snow. She sat up, bending her knees, and buried her face in her mitten-covered hands.

Enid cut across the frozen sea grass and hovered over the woman. "You're new. I wonder what your story is."

The woman's shoulders shook as she cried, ignoring Enid. "I won't let him do this to me, I won't do it." She stood, brushing snow off her legs, and stomped her boots on the ground. "That asshole doesn't deserve to be Shane's father, my son already has a dad." The woman muttered through choked sobs and gasping breaths, pacing down the hill toward the porch of the house.

"Who are we talking about?" Enid followed the hysterical woman as she yanked on the broken front door until it flung open so fast, she stumbled backward, catching herself against the porch railing. "Of course, you can't hear me or see me. I am nothing, floating around... nothing to no one." She trailed the woman into the house and up the winding staircase. "What are you doing in my house?"

As Enid approached the woman and moved through her, a chilling wave of despair consumed her, blurring her vision with a cloud of darkness that settled in her chest, fading as she stepped away from the woman. "What the hell happened to you?" Enid whispered.

The woman paused, gripping the railing. Her breaths misted in front of her as Enid focused on being human and stormed ahead. The floor creaked under her footsteps and the woman gasped, covering her mouth with her hands.

"You can't hear me, but you sure can hear when I move stuff, can't you?" Grabbing the bathroom door handle, Enid slammed it shut, sending the hanging light fixture in the hallway swinging. "Why doesn't this work in other places, like

Maddie and Drew's house?" She still had many unanswered questions about living as a dead person.

"This place is cursed." The woman sniffled as she spoke. She spun around in the hallway and reached inside her coat pocket, pulling out a small flashlight. A beam of light lit up the hallway as the woman hurried inside the last bedroom on the left.

"What are you doing in here?" Desperation coursed through Enid and her skin shimmered with an angelic glow as she paced around the woman.

The woman rummaged through the empty drawers of the worn dressers and an armoire that had been in Enid's home forever. "That son of a bitch won't strip my son of everything." Dropping to the edge of the bed, the woman covered her face, wailing. "How can no one see him for who he is? Lying, cheating, stealing, abusive... He made a fool out of me." The flashlight fell to the floor as she balled her hands into fists at her sides.

"Who?" Enid sat beside her and the woman glanced down, running her hand over the spot on the bed where Enid sat. "That's right, I live here. Keep talking, lady. I need to know what you want from my house."

Retrieving the flashlight, the woman shone it around the room, stopping at a jewelry box on the dresser. She lifted the lid, picking up Jack's gold pocket watch nestled among necklaces and earrings. With tears streaming over her cheeks, she pried open the decorative watch cover, turning it over in her hand. "I'm taking this so my boy has a piece of a family he'll never come to know," she said, tucking the watch in her pocket as she hurried toward the bedroom door to leave.

Enid rushed to stand in front of her, and the woman's breaths fogged between them, but the woman didn't seem to notice. Placing her hands on the woman's cheeks, Enid glared into her sad eyes. "This is my house, not yours. Give it back."

With trembling hands, the woman held the flashlight, sending light bouncing along the staircase down to the piano. "I know what he did." Her voice shook as she spoke. "I'm leaving town to keep my boy safe, but I will make sure everyone knows the truth when it's safe."

"You know?" Enid grasped the woman's shoulders, but her hands passed right through her. Spinning around, Enid faced the woman's back as she charged down the winding stairs, her boots echoing in the grand room. "Wait, don't go! If you know what he did and where he is, tell someone! Please, don't leave."

The front door slammed shut, and the house fell into its weary silence.

Enid charged downstairs, through the door and stood on the porch as the woman darted in a blur of snow up the hill to her car. Her broken soul begged for revenge... For peace. The scream caged inside her let go, but she couldn't hear herself or feel her chest move with the exhale, like she was being held underwater or suffocating. Dropping to her knees, her body flickered and a current of warmth pulsed through her as she faded into a calm void.

An intense light flashed as she glided through a strange void, landing with a cushioned fall. Gentle waves lapped around her with a warm embrace, extending beyond her skin to her very core, bathing her face in a radiant glow behind her closed eyes. She dragged her fingers along the ground beside her, gathering a fistful of sand. As she opened her eyes, she relaxed her hand, letting the sand escape through her fingers like time slipping away in an hourglass.

A shadow passed over her, blocking the sun, and she sat up. Aurora's flowing black hair held a purple glow as she hovered over her. "I must remove your choice to stay in wait." Her voice chimed like a haunting lullaby, sweet with a hint of power.

"What do you mean?" Enid leaped to her feet, and the sand fell off her like a magical hand had swept it away.

A smile crossed Aurora's scarred face as the vibrant purple light surrounded them. "Until she is of age to seek haven for you and for others, your pain becomes ours. Your roots run as deep as my own, and our destiny shall forever be intertwined. This allows me the power to help breathe life and peace for as long as you shall need it." Heartbreak crossed Aurora's eyes as her gaze shifted to the strange calm of the horizon. "I am afraid he has returned. However, there is nothing we can do now."

"You mean my brother, don't you?" Enid demanded. The sky transitioned from cobalt to violet, and a raven flew overhead, landing on a boulder. "Where are we?"

"In between the living and the dead." A smile brightened Aurora's sad eyes. "Paradise, as some will call it."

Enid dragged her feet through the sand, savoring the feeling of warmth as the grains shifted between her toes. She sauntered up to Aurora, where the surf rippled over the shore. The water swirled around her feet without touching them. "How long will I be here?"

"Until she is ready," Aurora said.

"Drew Harlow." Enid's hair brushed her chin, and she reveled in the soft strands against her face. This place surrounded her with overwhelming love, burying the sharp edges of sadness and anger. "Is this the timeless peace you keep talking about?"

"It is." Aurora raised her hands, and a sudden barrage of clouds rolled across the sky. A chain of lightning struck the sea as a beam of vibrant purple erupted from her palms and trailed the smoke rising from the water. A shiny object rose from the depths, swirling in a blur of silver across the surface, landing in Aurora's hands.

The amulet.

Aurora held the jewel up toward Enid, and a cluster of lights sparkled deep inside it. "The death of a mystic will ignite a fury from the other side so fierce the girl will require protection. You will be her messenger." With the amulet dangling from her fingers, Aurora placed her hands on Enid's face and chanted. "I summon thee, spirit of the sea, whose name bears light to guide those in need."

Enid's jaw tensed, and an explosion of fireworks sparked through her head, blurring her vision. As her eyes drifted closed, a vision of a young woman with fiery red hair walking through a hallway lined with lockers consumed her mind. Sneakers squeaked on tiled floors as students rushed past the girl, carrying books and backpacks. The vision flickered, and Enid's brother flashed, except he wasn't the Ben Morana she'd remembered. He was older, and everything about him was different; his hair, the way he dressed and carried himself as he strutted through a vast warehouse wearing a suit. If it weren't for the sinister glare in his dark eyes, she wouldn't have recognized him. The taste of metal filled Enid's mouth as Aurora removed her hands, ending the vision.

Stepping back, Enid dug her feet deeper into the sand. "What was that?"

"For as long as there will be others like us, there will be danger. His wrath will end with her. She is the only one who has the power to stop him forever. When her time arrives, call upon me, and I shall entrust you with the amulet laden with the Sisterhood's power."

"Her power isn't gone forever?" Enid clapped her hands, intertwining her fingers as her skin tingled. "Wait, she'll be in danger? How did Maddie know?" Enid plopped down in the sand. "So, Maddie was just trying to keep her safe."

Crouching beside her, Aurora's intense gaze locked with Enid's, rendering her helpless to look away. "All is not lost. Consequences will find him, and your tether to this world shall be broken. You will find your forever paradise, but until then, time does not exist here."

"What are you going to do to me?"

Aurora's eyes twinkled with flecks of purple and gold as she smiled. "I will do for you what her grandmother did for her."

Enid relaxed into the stoic feeling consuming her with a comforting peace. "My memories will be gone, too?" she said.

"It's the only way, until you are both ready." The waves rose to meet Aurora as she stood. The green in the trees lining the cliffs brightened against the sky, carrying the scent of wildflowers. Ribbons of purple light danced over the water as Aurora faded into a silhouette of mist, taking the amulet with her.

Calm surrounded Enid, and she lay back on the sand as a tingling sensation of warmth cascaded from the top of her head down to her toes. A profound stillness wrapped around her as her body faded into the earth, suspended in a beautiful nothingness.

Time didn't exist here, but time would pass for Drew Harlow, and Enid would be ready. This was only the beginning.

EPILOGUE

AURORA

Madeline Harlow had never regained her magical abilities, yet her granddaughter's gift to see beyond the veil to the other side had never left. The spell had worked, creating a barrier that blocked the Wandering Souls from Drew, but only for a short time, erasing the girl's memories of the dead ones bound to the amulet.

Enid.

Despite Aurora's warnings, Maddie overlooked the most important part of the spell, never uttering the words and casting her own magic away forever.

What you lose will come back again.

Standing on the beach the locals had named Jupiter Cove, Aurora kept her distance as Drew sat on a log of driftwood, staring into the night sky. The young woman's life remained untouched by the Sisterhood's magic, but its arrival was as certain as the storms gathering on the horizon.

Aurora had a promise to keep to Enid, and with Drew's eighteenth birthday approaching, they were both ready for their worlds to collide. Drew's fiery red hair whipped in her face, and she brushed strands away as Aurora glided closer, unseen. The young woman's grief was palpable in the air surrounding her, and Aurora approached, allowing Drew's pain to seep into her own being. A frigid weight gripped Aurora's chest, and she closed her eyes, wrapping her fingers around the amulet. Power awakened, coursing through her, offering a glimpse into the girl's heartache.

She had lost her first love.

Aurora trailed the mystical young woman as she hurried home and ascended the veranda steps. "He was not meant to be," she whispered in Drew's ear. "You are never alone, embrace your gift."

"Please, go away!" Drew's voice wavered as she spoke, and Aurora closed the gap between them, but an invisible wall radiated from the girl, hindering Aurora's calming magic.

"I mean you no harm," Aurora said.

Drew threw open the bright yellow door, the hinges squeaking in protest, and bolted inside, leaving Aurora alone with the rhythmic chirping of crickets.

Aurora's role was to guide with love, offer protection, and breathe life when darkness interfered with fate. Drew's journey of embracing her gift would feel solitary for the young woman, as Aurora had known all too well. She could never alter Drew's destined course, yet premonitions of danger lurked, and Aurora vowed not to stray far from her life.

Atlas Cliffs was a haven for mystics, and Drew Harlow would be no exception. Glimmers of hope in the abyss of darkness and love would surround the young woman as she left her mark on this town and a legacy of her own.

With a powerful beat of its wings, the raven soared near Aurora, landing on a lamppost across the coastal road. As she floated nearer, the raven's wingspan cast a long shadow under the silver glow of the moon.

We are never as alone as we may feel.

"We meet again," she said with a smile. "She will need our help."

With a curious tilt of its head, the raven watched Aurora as she crossed the veil, stepping into a world beyond the living.

281

Acknowledgements

I didn't plan on writing a prequel, but when I ended the Atlas Cliffs series with Braving Storms, something was missing. Maddie Harlow had her own story, and the only way I could share it was to write a book dedicated to giving her a voice. But as I wrote part one, another character wanted in on the journey, and a part two, including Enid Morana flowed onto the pages. Of course, it couldn't be *Aurora's Amulet* without the Atlas Cliffs original Mystic herself, and Aurora wove her way into the story, bringing Jack along with her.

Gigi's Creatives designed the beautiful cover for *Aurora's Amulet,* and her talent amazes me. I'm so grateful to have connected with you, Gigi. Thank you for unraveling the vision I had for this cover and turning it into art. I'm excited to work with her again in the coming months, creating the cover for my first adult contemporary, romantic suspense, *Shattered Secrets Between Us.*

I'm obsessed with character and bookish art, and that includes having unique chapter headers in my books. Thank you, Whitney Law, for drawing images capturing the essence of Maddie and Enid. Up next are chapter headers for my romantic suspense couple, Francesca, aka 'Frankie' Roscoe, and Rhett Marshall. I love our brainstorms, the sketch "doodles" you send me, and those moments when your creativity takes over and you just get it beautifully perfect.

A special thank you always to Kayla Ramoutar for being the editor I need for these stories. You push me a step further, reminding me of my "Angela-isms" when I need to step back and let my characters have their own voice. Thanks for seeing this entire series through with me.

My author path always has me venturing outside my comfort zone, and with encouragement from author friends and the support of readers, I created an official author team. Thank you to my ARC/Street Team of dedicated readers. Friendships have developed, and I appreciate you so much. I'll never stop saying it. You mean the world to me.

Thank you to Sara Flanagan, Tess Watters, Jaclyn Kot, and Krista Scott for listening, celebrating the wins, supporting me through the speed bumps, and just being my friend when I've needed one.

To my family. Thanks for supporting me when I need to escape into my writing cave, immersing myself in fictional worlds when real life is always happening around us, and loving me no matter what. And Roman, thank you for helping me brainstorm bad guys for my next book as I talk about the entire plot and characters like they're real people... Book characters have a way of doing that to writers, what can I say.

Thank you to the readers who continue to take a chance on me and my books. I couldn't keep doing this without you... *seriously*, I couldn't. I adore you so much!

Well, the Atlas Cliffs series is a wrap. That's it, she's done... well unless one day I decide to write a, 'where are they now' story... but for now, there are new characters excited to meet you. Until next time!

Your author friend,

Angela

Also by Angela van Liempt

Launch into Drew Harlow's mystical journey.
The Atlas Cliffs series

Angela van Liempt is a small-town girl with big dreams. Music inspires her and she creates a playlist for every book she writes. The Atlas Cliffs series emerged from her curiosity with the paranormal, but along the way, she discovered a passion for weaving romance into her stories.

She lives in Atlantic Canada with her family and her beloved dog, Harley, otherwise known as 'Pippy' or 'Harley-Quinn'. A lover of the ocean, full moons, and sunsets, she'd choose to be barefoot on a beach any day over big city life. Escaping into fictional coastal towns with characters who feel like real people is one of her favorite pastimes.

Follow for writing updates, book playlists and more!
https://www.dawn-publishing.com/
https://linktr.ee/angeladvl